BEACH HOME BEGINNINGS

CLIFFSIDE POINT

ELLEN JOY

For Diane, thank you for being the best mother-in-law I could ask for. You're a strong role model who I've always admired. And thanks for the meatballs.

ALSO BY ELLEN JOY

Click HERE for more information about other books by Ellen Joy.

New Hopes in the Valley

Feeling Blessed in the Valley

<u>Blueberry Bay</u>

The Cottage at Blueberry Bay

The Market at Blueberry Bay

Beach Rose Secrets

CHAPTER 1

*E*velyn looked around the ferry and felt old—really old. A sea of gray-headed bodies had gathered on the top floor of the ferry as they admired the view of the Atlantic Ocean, and for the first time, she felt her age. No one looked a day younger than fifty, and at fifty-five, she didn't feel as old as they all looked. But like most of the women on the ferry, her dyed hair didn't fool anyone. Most of the middle-aged men wore boat shoes and polo shirts, along with visors and readers. Worse, she was pretty sure Wanda, a stranger who hadn't stopped talking for the first twenty minutes of the forty-five-minute ferry ride, was not trying to mingle with the opposite sex like the brochure promoted. Evelyn didn't come to mingle with a sixty-two-year-old female divorcée from Palm Springs. She came to prove her sister wrong.

"I love to travel. Do you travel?" Wanda asked Evelyn.

Evelyn grinned but scanned to see if there were men on the ferry. Talk about false advertising. She peeked around through the seats, checking out the gray heads and seeing some light reflecting off bald scalps.

Dang Carol.

Even now, her sister still bossed her into this single-and-mingle tour on Martha's Vineyard. Seven days and six nights on the island. They started at the ferry port in Falmouth Harbor, where she first got stuck talking to Wanda about traveling, and she hadn't spent a single moment mingling with singles in the middle of the Atlantic Ocean.

"Africa was my favorite." Wanda held a dramatic pause for questioning.

"It must've been lovely," Evelyn said back, but really, she'd heard enough of the luxurious African trip.

"I saw a few lionesses on my safari, but no lions." Wanda pulled out her phone and opened her pictures. "You can't really see it, but there's a giraffe way off in the distance."

"I'm going to use the restroom," Evelyn said, pointing to the staircase. "Then probably get a breath of fresh air."

She noticed a few men standing at what looked like a coffee bar. "Need anything?"

Wanda picked up her purse. "You know, I should take a tinkle as well."

Evelyn moaned silently. She didn't mind meeting new people —it didn't have to be just men—but she needed to meet *a man*, then she could buzz off and do her own thing which was write. Just like always. Then when she got home and her sister asked for details, she could report back with a real man she could look up and show off. Evelyn wasn't dead like her husband; she could get out there. She chose not to because, well, she didn't really like people all that much.

After George had died, she'd wanted to talk about him, talk about his sudden death, and that made people uncomfortable, especially men his own age. A heart attack, just like that? Fit George? At fifty? No signs? His death proved it could happen to anyone.

People didn't like to talk about death. They didn't want to face the idea of mortality. Evelyn faced it every day. Alone.

She had her girls, but they were in their twenties and had their own lives. She had Carol, of course, but her sister hadn't stopped

2

trying to set her up since she'd passed Emily Post's timeline of grief. She meant well, but it was also attached to her mental health check-in. Apparently, she wasn't old enough to stop being interested in the opposite sex after becoming a widow. At her age, she should still want to date. She should want to move on and find love again. If she didn't, something must be wrong with her.

"Don't you think he'd want you to move on?" Carol had asked her as she gave Evelyn the trip.

Evelyn had no idea what George would've wanted. They'd never talked about it. She'd never thought he just wouldn't come home one day. How many times had she heard people's stories on the morning news shows? They always said, "It was just a regular day."

And it *was* just a regular day. She hadn't even said goodbye that afternoon when he went out to run an errand. She became annoyed when he hadn't come home on time. She had been working on her best novel yet and didn't want to be interrupted. Not to mention he was late for dinner, and she was starving. When the police had shown up, she still couldn't comprehend what was happening. She remembered worrying there might be a burglary in the neighborhood.

"Ma'am, there's been an accident."

They said he hadn't known anything had happened; he'd died that quick. The heart attack had luckily only caused him to steer off the road, and no one else was involved. Everyone said something must've been looking out for them.

But how could someone be looking out for her if they'd taken her husband in one fell swoop?

Now she was stuck with Wanda following her to the restroom.

"I'm going to stop and get coffee," Evelyn said, trying to ditch the redhead.

"Oh, I'd love some," she said, digging in her purse and handing Evelyn a twenty. "Get two!"

Wanda shuffled off to the restroom as Evelyn stood dumb-founded, staring at the twenty.

"I sat next to her on the plane," a man's voice said from behind her, which made Evelyn jump.

"Oh, my goodness gracious!" She placed her hand on her chest, recovering her breath from the startle. She looked back to see a tall man with salt-and-pepper hair standing in line for coffee.

He extended his hand. "Mitch."

"Evelyn," she said back, taking his hand in hers. At first glance, Mitch was extremely handsome and seemed to understand her dilemma with Wanda. "You flew in from Palm Springs?"

He nodded. "Two flights. We must've used the same travel agent, because they booked our seats like we were a couple."

"Wow." She was impressed he was only drinking coffee.

"Had breakfast together at the hotel this morning, even." He looked at the bathroom in fear. "I've been trying to avoid her this whole ride."

"Good luck," she said. "Let me know how you do."

He chuckled. "Looks like you need the luck."

He nodded as Wanda came out of the bathroom, then disappeared in the crowd as soon as he got his coffee. As Evelyn stood in line, she tried to remember his name. *Martin? No, Mitch. That's it.* She could tell her sister his name was Mitch and he lived in Palm Springs. Real person. Check.

Before he slipped away from the creamer, she asked, "So, what do you do in Palm Springs?"

He poured the cream and then looked up at her. "I'm in real estate."

Occupation: real estate. Check.

She didn't even bother to ask another question.

Wanda came back as promised, and the two women decided to go up on the top deck.

"Oh, there's Mitch!" Wanda waved her arm up in the air as Mitch stood talking to a group of people.

He waved back but winked to Evelyn. She smiled, holding back her eye roll at the cheesy gesture, but steered Wanda away to the other end of the ferry. "I don't want to sit in the sun."

"Oh, you're right. I shouldn't be in the hot sun either."

From inside her purse, Wanda pulled out a flexible visor with the widest bill Evelyn had ever seen.

"Wow."

"I know, isn't it great?" Wanda adjusted the back around her curls. "Doesn't let any of the sun in."

Evelyn took out her extra-large pair of prescription sunglasses and put them on.

"Those are nice as well," Wanda said, nodding in approval.

Evelyn gestured toward a bench up close to the railing. "How about there?"

"Perfect." Wanda didn't waste any time claiming the bench, hurrying her petite body over to the edge of the ferry. Wanda reminded Evelyn of a Talbots' mannequin. She wore a soft pastel knit sweater, hanging around her shoulders with a matching sleeveless knit shirt, khakis, and sensible sandals. The two sat and looked out at the water. The gray sea seemed endless.

"You can see whales out here sometimes," she said loudly to Wanda over the ferry's engine. She had seen dozens when she used to travel to the island as a young twenty-year-old. The whales could be spotted from the ferries, but with her luck, they'd run across some environmental hazard.

"Where did you travel from?" Wanda asked.

"Minnesota." She didn't offer more. Evelyn didn't have it in her to talk about the home where she spent more than twenty years with her husband.

Wanda began to tell her about her experiences in Minneapolis, starting with the Mall of America. "I couldn't believe there's an actual roller coaster inside. And there's this underwater world. Plus, the lakes out there . . . Some look as big as this!"

Wanda drew her arms out toward the ocean water, then fell

quiet. And for a brief moment, the two sat quietly. Evelyn breathed in the tangy air and held it in her lungs. She had forgotten the smell.

"Sorry if I'm clinging to you," Wanda said.

Evelyn jerked back. Had her face showed her annoyance? "Oh, you're not clingy!"

Wanda motioned her head to the inside of the ferry. "I saw you talking to Mitch at the coffee bar, and I'm pretty sure he's been avoiding me."

Evelyn's heart dropped as Wanda's eyes moistened.

"I was trying to mingle like the brochure said." Wanda pretended to laugh, but her bottom lip wobbled.

Evelyn froze. She was horrible in these kinds of situations. Did she reach out and offer comfort? And what exactly would that look like?

"It's been so long since my divorce, you know?" Wanda dug into her purse, pulling out a tissue. "Ugh, sorry. I'm a mess."

Just as Wanda blew her nose, a seagull cried out, catching Evelyn's attention. It flew in the air as if racing the ferry to the island, showing off its aerodynamics and sailing in the wind.

Oh, George, she thought. Her overly friendly husband would have encouraged Evelyn to help comfort this stranger. Always a healer; it was why he became a doctor. He'd wanted to help. He'd wanted to comfort and care for people. But Evelyn wasn't George. She didn't know how to help others, because she couldn't even help herself. It had been five years since George died, and she still couldn't face his death. She still lived her life as if he was going to walk through the front door from his errand at any moment. She hadn't moved on, and she was certain she never would.

But suddenly the seagull dropped onto the ferry's railing, and she swore it stared at her.

Fine. I'll be nice.

Evelyn shifted her position and faced Wanda. She didn't know

much about the strange woman besides she liked the act of gabbing, but she did empathize with her.

She took a deep breath and said, "I lost my husband five years ago, and my sister thinks if I take this trip, I'll be able to let go and move on. So, *my plan* was to get the name of a living person for my sister's benefit, then sit in my hotel all day. Mitch was that living person."

"You must've been devastated," Wanda said. "Losing your husband."

"He died of a heart attack." Evelyn braced herself for the pounding of pain, the sudden realization she'd never see George again, or hear his deep voice, or feel his sweet warmth, or smell his beautiful scent. But it didn't come.

"I'm so sorry." Wanda's demeanor changed; her antsy movements and chitter-chatter stopped. Evelyn recognized the look in her eyes because she had seen it in her own—the pain of loss.

Evelyn immediately looked for the seagull, but it had left, and that's when the familiar wave of grief washed over her like it did these days, completely out of nowhere. She grabbed the bench's arm, squeezing it as she waited for the intensity to dissipate. Five years may seem like a long time, but in death, it felt like yesterday. Time didn't heal. Time just moved on, and her husband was still dead.

Maybe her sister was right. Maybe she did die a little bit with George.

God, she missed George.

"I'm sorry about your divorce," she said back to Wanda, hoping to bring back the chatty woman.

"Thanks." Wanda's voice sounded melancholy. She stood up, holding her purse in her arms. "I should go find a new seat."

"What for?" Evelyn asked.

"I've been bothering you enough," Wanda said.

"Nonsense." Evelyn patted the empty spot. "You haven't told me the story about the lightning. You know, when you were doing water aerobics."

Wanda's face lit up, and she immediately took back her place. She held up her hands like a conductor ready to start in on a long composition, and began, "All of us ladies have water aerobics on Tuesdays at eight, and this is the desert, so when we saw the clouds, we weren't concerned . . ."

The rest of the ride, Wanda told Evelyn about her home in an over fifty-five retirement community of thousands.

"What is it like to never see kids around?" Evelyn asked. She didn't know how she felt about living in a community like that.

"It's nice to have people around you. You know, going through everything together." Wanda shrugged her shoulders. "I know if I don't pick up my newspaper at six, my neighbor's going to notice and check in on me."

Evelyn agreed with a nod. She understood that. "My daughters don't think about checking in. Not that they have to—they're adults, after all—but if I choke on a hoagie, there's no one there."

This had been her fear since losing George. What if she had a heart attack herself? She didn't want to die alone. The fact so many of the health officials told her George was lucky to die so quickly made her think her chances of that happening were low. She didn't want to be that person—lying on the floor for days until someone sees the mail piled up.

"The only negative is that conversations revolve around illnesses and death." Wanda shook her head. "It's how I feel about social media too. Nothing good comes from that kind of talk." She shifted in her seat and tapped Evelyn's elbow. "Let's get a better view."

Up ahead, she could see the shores of Martha's Vineyard starting to come into focus. In the harbor, tiny sailboats scattered the water. Large mansions, dressed in the Vineyard's gray clapboard, dotted the shoreline. One thing she hadn't forgotten was the beauty of the island.

"Our first stop is . . ." Wanda pulled out her itinerary.

"How much do you have in there?" Evelyn teased about Wanda's luggage-sized purse.

"Everything." Wanda winked, and Evelyn realized she had misjudged Wanda.

"Would you like to sit together for lunch?" she asked.

Wanda hesitated. "Just the two of us?"

Evelyn had forgotten the point of the trip. "I mean, with whoever wants to join us."

"Think you could ask Mitch to join us?" she asked, her eyebrow raising.

Evelyn swung around to the coffee bar, where she last saw Mitch. There he was, now talking to a woman in a slim-fitting casual linen dress.

"He seems willing to talk to everyone." Evelyn observed. "Maybe we should see what else is out there."

"Good idea." Wanda shook her finger up to the sky. "Your sister's right. You should get out there."

As the ferry docked at the port, Evelyn looked out at the familiar harbor town that looked exactly like it had all those years ago.

"We can't check into the hotel for another couple hours," Wanda said, reading from the detailed packet. "They have a few suggestions for restaurants and shops."

"Let's hit the ladies' room before we get off the ferry." Evelyn shuffled them through the crowd as they made their way to the bathroom.

Evelyn left the bathroom first and waited for Wanda. She looked out at the tiny village the locals called Eastport. It wasn't the same size as the other ports on Martha's Vineyard—much smaller in comparison but had the same feel. It was maybe even more quaint, if that was possible. She inhaled the briny air, and memories instantly flooded back from thirty years ago.

As she calculated all the summers she spent in Martha's Vineyard back in college, she thought of him and tried to picture what he might look like now.

God, she thought, *thirty years ago.*

All those days at the beach and nights working at The Wharf.

Those had been the best summers of her life—all her hopes and dreams right before her. That's when she saw the sign: Martha's Mystery Book Shoppe. She stared at the simple clapboard building and its huge picture window with books displayed.

Would he still be on Martha's Vineyard?

She thought about ditching Wanda for a split second but fought against it as Wanda squeezed her petite body through the crowd and back to Evelyn. "They really need better soap in the bathrooms."

"Let's go to that bookstore," Evelyn said, pointing to the store as they disembarked the ferry. "We have a half hour to kill before the restaurant is even open."

"Sure, it's adorable." Wanda put her visor back on. "I should get a few books to read."

Wanda ushered her along to the exit as the ferry came to a stop. They followed the group to the port's station and out onto the road, which was filled with tourist businesses all along the strip. Site-seeing buses sat ready to go around the island, whale-watching adventures were only thirty dollars, and local restaurants and pubs lined the streets.

Evelyn didn't know what made her go. It would be like opening Pandora's Box; there would be no turning back. The minute she stepped into the bookstore, she'd be entering the past. Was she ready for what she might find?

She and Wanda waded through the crowd and crossed the street. She opened the door, and a bell dinged along its glass. Walking inside the shop, she stopped at the threshold and inhaled the familiar smell of new and old pages blended together. She hadn't forgotten the smell. It was her kind of mingling. She loved a bookstore, or a library, or a good reading nook—or any space with lots and lots of books.

She loved reading books as much as she loved writing them.

Ever since she was a little girl, she had written stories—fairy tales, animal adventures, action-adventures. She loved the escape of one's world. Everyone thought George's death had made her

stop writing, but she never stopped. She wrote every day. Sometimes, all day.

But not the stories Evelyn Rose wrote.

No, Evelyn Rose was the one who died with George.

The door behind her opened, and more tourists streamed in, moving her further inside the store. She checked out the titles on the display table that was front and center. There were old titles and classic authors like Steinbeck and Angelou, but new authors as well.

"I thought this would only be mysteries because of the name," a woman said behind them.

Evelyn's nerves rattled as she walked deeper into the store, waiting to see him. Wanda moved around to the other side of Evelyn, and in trying to stay out of the way, she bumped into another display case behind her. Books tumbled off, making a loud commotion and gaining everyone's attention.

She bent down and started picking up the books, when someone crouched down beside her, gathering up the ones out of her reach.

"Thank you so much," she said as she looked over at him. She almost dropped the books again. "Charlie."

He smiled, as if running into her for the first time in a very long time, wasn't a big deal. "Hello, Evelyn."

CHAPTER 2

*T*he morning Evelyn came into his bookstore, Charlie had just found his Aunt Martha's journal hidden in a dresser in her office. The tattered leather book had been a legend for him and his cousins, but no one had seen it since their childhood. His aunt, who'd never had children of her own, had supposedly written down the tales of their great-something-grandfather telling where he'd believed there was buried treasure. No one knew if the tales were true, but the real journal sat in his hands.

He had been cleaning out a closet, stuffed to the brim of Martha's things, including the dresser, which was also stuffed. His aunt had passed away last winter, and he had just recently started going through her things. He owed everything to the aunt who had raised him, given him a job and a place to live, and helped raise his daughter when he was a single dad. How could he get rid of her prize possessions? Especially since he might find buried treasure.

"Harper!" he yelled down the hall. "I found it!"

He rushed down toward the floor of the bookstore, where his daughter watched the front counter.

But his heart stopped dead cold when he saw her walk in.

Evelyn Flannery was back.

The look on her face reminded him of the first time he met her. She had been in college—hopeful, eager, and curious. Never in a million years would he have expected to see her again. And she looked great. Practically the same. He wished he could say the same. He had gained an extra few pounds over the years and a few more gray hairs. Not that he looked horrible, he hoped. He still enjoyed exercising and took care of himself. Besides, when did he start caring about the way he looked?

The minute he saw her again.

Evelyn Flannery. After all this time.

Well, not Flannery—Rose. She had become a Rose after marrying George. God, he was glad there wasn't social media back then.

Here and there, he'd hear some news about her, mostly in magazines and editorials. *"Evelyn Rose hits the New York Times' Best Sellers once again."* Book after book, year after year. Her commercial success had been so big that she had a television series. He didn't even know how many titles she had at this point.

She still had the same slim figure. Her blond hair was just as silky as before, even with the few grays. She practically looked twenty-five.

When she backed into his display case, he assumed she had seen him and spooked out, but he realized she hadn't when her face turned ashen like she had seen a ghost.

"Hello, Evelyn."

"Charlie." Her mouth stayed open as she gawked at him.

The woman next to her elbowed her. "Is this another guest on our tour?" She checked him out.

He reached out to collect the hardcovers from her hands. "What are you doing back on Martha's Vineyard?"

She looked around, scanning the room as if she were looking for someone else to jump out from behind the shelves.

"Do you still work here?" she asked.

He wasn't sure if her voice was filled with disappointment,

complete shock, or a mixture of both. "I do. It's my store now. Martha passed a few months ago."

"Oh." Her face dropped. "I'm so sorry."

"Thanks." He scanned the store thinking about how much had changed, if anything. What did she think of it?

"It still looks great," she said, as if reading his thoughts. She bent over and picked up the last of the titles on the floor and put them back on the display. "I'm really sorry about this."

"Are you staying in town?" he asked, hoping to catch her for longer. God, she looked great. She wore her hair down, just a little past her shoulders, and a headband held it back, helping the strands look casual but styled.

She nodded. "For about a week. How long have you been back on the island?"

Her friend's head tilted with every question, clearly listening to the whole conversation.

"I've been here twenty-one years."

He could tell she was calculating the dates in her head. The last time they saw each other was practically in the same spot. He waited for the inevitable questions about Tanya and his writing career.

"I tried getting in touch with you when you won that award you had talked about," he said.

"The RITA."

"Yes, that's it." He felt like a complete jerk, even if it was thirty years ago. "Are you here with George?"

"Are you and Tanya still married?" she said right back.

He felt the sting. She still held some feelings after all this time.

"We divorced." He could feel the *told you so*, but when silence permeated the space, he said, "It's good to see you, Evelyn." He pointed to the register, where a group of tourists stood in line. "I need to help the counter, but we should catch up sometime."

"Sure, that sounds nice." She gave a nod but stayed where she was. "Good to see you."

But he wasn't sure if she meant it, because the Evelyn he knew wore her heart on her sleeve. The Evelyn standing in front of him wore armor made of steel. He waved as he left toward the register, praying his daughter wouldn't notice Evelyn, the conversation, or catch on to his anxiety running up his chest and onto his neck. He could feel the heat rising from underneath his collar.

"What's with you?" Harper asked. Her eyebrow raised in early suspicion.

"Nothing. Why?"

She looked behind him, then around him, and then the other way.

"What?" he asked, wondering if he had something hanging out of his nose or . . . He checked his fly. Nope, not his zipper.

That's when the friend with the curly, wild hair came from around the corner with a stack of old mysteries that hung in the back from a mid-list cozy mystery author named Debra Collins. He wondered if Evelyn noticed he didn't carry her books.

"Evelyn Rose?" Harper's mouth dropped.

He flinched, realizing not telling her may be worse than giving her a heads-up.

"I can't believe it." Harper stepped out from behind the counter and over to Evelyn. "I love your work."

"Oh, that's nice." Evelyn held one of his handmade journals in her hand, one with a leather cover and no design. She blushed but didn't invite more conversation with his daughter.

"I've read almost every one of your books." Harper started rattling off titles of Evelyn's romances—books he didn't allow in the house, or the store, but that Aunt Martha fed her. "I've reread *Better with You* like twenty times."

He didn't want to think of his twenty-eight-year-old daughter reading romances written by the woman he'd once thought he'd spend the rest of his life with.

"That was one of my firsts," Evelyn said. "My first RITA Award winner."

"I love to write too."

"You write?" the friend asked, but to Evelyn, not Harper.

Evelyn hesitated, and Charlie realized the friend had no idea who Evelyn was. Her smile was abashed. "Yes, I'm a writer."

"She's an Oprah Book Club author," he said.

The friend's eyes widened at the mere mention of Oprah. "You met Oprah."

Evelyn shook her head. "No, I wish. I was just part of this promotion from her book club. Nothing crazy." She tilted her head at the stack of books still not rung up. "We need to get going."

"Oh jeez. Sorry." Harper ran back around the counter and started ringing up the mysteries. "Are you in town visiting?"

He waited for Evelyn's response.

"For the week," she said.

For the week, he thought.

"My dad said you got your big break right out of college," Harper said.

Evelyn glanced at him and then said, "Well, sort of."

"Any advice from a world-famous author?" he said, bagging up the books.

"Finish the book before you start worrying about anything else," Evelyn said.

"I've been revising my book with a critique group, but it's slow going since we meet only once a week." Harper's eyes widened in a quick realization.

Oh no, he thought, *please don't invite her to—.*

"You should come to our writer's group tonight," Harper said. "We'd love to have you join us."

"Oh, I don't think Ms. Rose wants to come to a writer's group on her vacation," Charlie said.

"I'd love to purchase a book from my new author friend, Evelyn." The redhead waited for Harper to take her credit card. Charlie stepped in front of his daughter and took the Platinum card from her manicured nails and rang it through.

"We're sold out," he answered before Harper made a fool out

of him. He didn't carry her books because he was like a lovesick kid who never got over his first true love.

"You're that famous?" The woman looked shocked and thrilled.

But Evelyn wasn't buying it. Her eyes slanted a bit, and this time, he could read her. Her angry look hadn't changed that was for sure.

"Good seeing you," he said, waving a goodbye with the receipt.

"Yes," she said back, but her focus was on Harper. "Good luck with the writing."

"Please think about it," Harper said. He loved his overly friendly daughter, but he silently wished she'd stop talking.

His heart started pounding as Evelyn stood there, silent.

"Sure," Evelyn finally said. "I'd love to."

"Seriously?" Harper's eyes widened. "That's great. We meet at seven, we always have wine and a good time."

Evelyn dug into her purse and pulled out a card. "This is my assistant. Send her a copy of your manuscript to the email address here, explain that we talked, and I'll make sure to read it and give you a few pointers."

Charlie's racing heart started beating faster, and Harper was speechless for the first time in her life.

"That's really kind of you—" he began to say, "but you're on vacation."

Evelyn's gaze went back to Charlie, and her eyes hooked into his, a feeling so familiar washed through him like a wave before a storm. Suddenly, emotions swirled inside of him he hadn't felt in years.

"We should get going," Evelyn said.

He realized he had been staring when she tugged at her friend. Evelyn turned and left before he could say anything.

Charlie watched as Evelyn disappeared into the crowd along the sidewalk down Harbor Lane.

Harper flipped the card with her fingers. "Do you think she came here to see you?"

Charlie had no idea why Evelyn would come into the bookstore after all these years.

"She's married, and happily, as I recall." He had heard from a few friends here and there that she had married a doctor, moved back home to the Midwest, and had two kids and a dog.

"She's not wearing a ring," Harper noted, playing around on her phone.

That surprised him. Last he'd heard, they'd been together for years. Had they divorced?

"Oh, he died." Harper flung her phone in his face. "Look."

"America's favorite romance author loses the love of her life."

Love of her life? Where did he fit on the scale of things? She looked as though she couldn't get out of there fast enough. He did, however, feel sorry she had lost George. He hadn't met him, but from what some of their friends had said, he sounded like a solid guy; someone who deserved happiness with Evelyn.

God knows she deserved some after what Charlie did to her.

CHAPTER 3

*I*t was the dang New England accent that made her knees wobbly. Did she look like a complete idiot just standing there with her tongue hanging out of her mouth? How could he look even better thirty years later? Did he resemble Colin Firth, or was it just her?

"Is it hot out?" she asked, using a book from Wanda's pile to fan herself. They had reached the hotel where they were staying. A crowd from the tour stood around in the lobby, waiting for the luncheon.

"Honey, it's wicked," another woman said with a heavy drawl. She sat on a bench in a sunhat, sundress, and freshly painted sun-kissed toes. "You ladies on the tour?" The woman bobbed her foot up and down as her flip-flop bopped along, hanging onto her foot. "I can't take this humidity." She continued pulling her collar away from her neck. "I thought the summers here were mild."

"It can get warm when the air is still," Evelyn said, remembering the days of waiting tables, praying she didn't sweat through her shirt. The summers with . . .

"Who was the man you were talking to?" Wanda asked Evelyn.

"Oh, an old acquaintance."

"Seemed more than an old acquaintance," Wanda said back.

"I hardly even recognized him." It was a lie; mostly for herself. The way Charlie carried himself—his quiet demeanor, his stoic voice—washed feelings loose inside her. Feelings she hadn't recovered from. Feelings that once had a leak that almost drowned her. And she was still drowning from George.

Why had she agreed to this trip?

"He seemed nervous," Wanda pointed out, but Evelyn hadn't seen that. Maybe a little bit unsure how to deal with seeing her, but not nervous.

The woman on the bench shifted her position, listening in on their conversation. Evelyn checked her phone again. The girls still hadn't texted back from her text this morning letting them know she arrived at the island. She didn't expect them to respond right away, but maybe a thumbs-up? Something. "We should hit the restaurant."

"Y'all mind if I tag along?" the woman asked, her drawl thick.

Wanda shot a look at Evelyn as if waiting to see her thoughts about including this newcomer.

"Not at all," Evelyn answered for them. Hopefully, she'll distract Wanda from asking more questions. "Where did you travel from?"

"Oklahoma." The woman reached out her hand, full of large silver turquoise jewelry that dazzled in the sunlight. "Barbara Lightfoot, but everyone calls me Bitty."

Evelyn wasn't sure if the nickname was ironic or not, but Bitty stood almost six feet tall if she had to guess.

"My daddy used to call me it when I was an itty-bitty thing." She used her hand to show how high she'd stood at the time.

Evelyn smiled, putting the tidbit in her mental file folder, a clever habit she developed as a kid. Little nuances people did as she observed. Tiny pieces of information about someone's personal life. Things she could later use for a character or story idea. George was her biggest muse when it came to human behaviors. He'd bounce his knee when he read the paper, hum when he yawned, and he scraped the last of the peanut butter with his middle finger to get as far to the bottom as possible.

She wondered if Charlie noticed his mannerisms written within the pages of her books, or if he had even read her "silly little romances."

She sighed and realized that both women were looking at her. "Did I miss something?"

"I missed your last name?" Bitty said.

"Oh, I'm sorry. It's Rose. My name is Evelyn Rose."

"Well, I'll be. I thought that was you." Bitty smiled wide at Evelyn like they were old friends. "I went and saw you at the Dallas Romance Conference."

Evelyn smiled at the coincidence. Wanda's mouth opened wide as she looked back and forth between the two women.

"That was about six years ago, right?" Evelyn hadn't been to another conference since George. Would she get the fan turnout as she once had? Her readers were now older women. Women who had grown through motherhood and middle age with Evelyn.

"What do you write?" Wanda still appeared confused.

"Honey, this isn't just any old romance writer." Bitty chuckled. "Well, shoot. Now I'm on this singles tour, and all I want to do is talk to my favorite author." Bitty turned to Wanda and said, "She wrote The Vineyard Series, the one on Netflix." Bitty pulled out her phone, but Evelyn stopped her.

"I write mostly romance." Evelyn didn't really want to talk about writing. Not that she needed to hide. At first, people found it interesting, but then they'd run out of questions and recognize that it's not as glamourous as other famous professions. Writing at three in the morning isn't exactly an attractive lifestyle.

"Are you here to talk about romance?" Bitty asked. "Or are you looking for an idea for your next book?"

Evelyn laughed as if Bitty had made a joke. The irony that she, a romance writer, was on a trip looking for fake romance didn't escape her. "No, just here as a guest. You could say my sister thought I was becoming stale and needed a wake-up vacation."

Bitty nodded as if she understood. "Well, I don't know about you girls, but I'm starving."

Evelyn heard her own stomach grumble. "I'm pretty hungry myself."

Wanda pulled out the tour's itinerary and pointed at the restaurant's menu. "We're eating at the hotel's lunch buffet in the ocean view room, which looks out at . . ."

"The Vineyard Sound," Evelyn answered for her.

"It says here there's going to be an oyster bar." Wanda made a face. "I just hate oysters."

Memories flooded back to Evelyn as the three women walked down the wide wooden front porch and into the main dining room. Years ago, the inside had been dark with an interior that resembled the inside of a luxurious yacht. Now, the space had been opened to a grand spiral staircase with a wall of windows facing the Atlantic Ocean. A stone fireplace anchored the room, standing at least three stories tall. The rock surround looked like it had been tumbled in the ocean, along with the twelve-foot piece of driftwood used as the mantle. The changes were drastic, yet perfect. It looked magnificent.

Wanda held up her finger and pointed to the bathroom. "I'm going to piddle."

"I'm going to make a stop as well," Bitty said, following Wanda.

Evelyn peeked into the bar area. Soft music played in the background as people mingled with one another. Not wanting to go in without her sudden new friends, she stayed in the shadows of the hallway. Two hours ago, she was ready to ditch Wanda, and now she was frozen in place, not willing to venture into a room without her. Even if the room was filled with people who wanted to meet people.

What would George think of this whole scenario?

"Hey, you."

She swung around to see Mitch standing behind her. He must've just used the restroom, because she hadn't seen him come from the front door.

"Are you alone?" he asked, looking around.

At first, she didn't know what he was referring to, but he whispered, "Is Wanda with you?"

She understood the woman could talk, but he was being rude at this point. "Yes, she's in the restroom."

"You can't get away?"

Guilt sat in her stomach. "She's actually quite lovely."

He grimaced. "How about you join me for lunch?"

She could see Wanda and Bitty coming out of the restroom together.

"Thanks, but I already planned to eat with Wanda and Bitty."

Wanda's face brightened right away when she saw Mitch standing next to Evelyn, but Bitty's scowled.

"Well, if it isn't Mitch," Bitty said.

"You know Mitch?" Wanda asked in surprise.

"Yes, I know him." Bitty looked down at him.

Mitch appeared flustered suddenly. "Bitty, good to see you again."

Bitty may be from Oklahoma, but she looked more like a retired Dallas Cowboy cheerleader. With her height, and her bra size, she was a bombshell. Evelyn wasn't at all surprised that Mitch had introduced himself to her.

"I should grab myself a table," he said, scooting away.

Wanda raised her hand as though she wanted to get his attention, but he was already out of earshot.

"Did that man hit on all of us in less than twenty-four hours?" Bitty asked as they sat down at a seat. The table sat high on a deck that overlooked the harbor. Sailboats dotted the port, tethered to buoys. The water appeared like glass in between the boats, reflecting off the different-colored hulls.

"He tried to get me to"—Wanda used air quotes—"watch a movie last night."

Bitty slapped her hand against her chest. "He did not. Heavens to Betsy, that man moves fast."

Wanda's eyes widened in horror. "I think I would've gone, too, if I hadn't taken that sleeping pill."

Evelyn almost spit out her water as she laughed. Wanda was not at all what she had originally expected.

Wanda shrugged. "What? I came here for a singles vacation. Isn't that what this is all about?"

"I hope to God not." Evelyn hadn't thought *that* was on the table. What had her sister gotten her into?

"Hold up a moment." Bitty held up her hand. "First, let's address the fact that this is just a group of adults that are looking for consensual relationships. Second, you would've slept with that guy?"

Wanda thought for a moment and then shrugged again. "Well, I haven't been with another man since I married Bill."

Evelyn had never been so glad she'd been wrong about a person than she had been with Wanda.

"I think it's your choice. You're sixty-two for goodness' sake," Evelyn said. "But maybe not someone like Mitch?"

"I want to be dazzled before anything happens. Holding my hand is more than a dinner out. I want to be wined and dined and jeweled well before any of that." Bitty leaned back in her seat and looked over the menu. "You ladies like a margarita?"

Wanda checked her phone. "It's only noon."

Evelyn hadn't had a drink at noon since before marrying George. With two kids at home, she couldn't even think of having a drink during the day. But she didn't have a two-year-old or four-year-old now. She quickly checked her own phone. No messages. No one to call and no one calling her. She could be dead, and no one would be the wiser. "Let's do it!"

"Thatta girl." Bitty raised her hand at the waiter. "Excuse me!"

A young gentleman came to their table, no pad in hand. "Can I get you ladies something to drink?"

Bitty looked at the waiter. "We'd love your best house margarita."

"We have a cucumber margarita with triple sec, lime—"

"We'll take three," Evelyn ordered and handed him a card. "And your biggest sample platter of apps."

"Thanks, girl," Bitty said, kicking her flip-flop up and down as she sat back in her chair, adjusting her sunhat to shade her eyes.

"You're welcome," Evelyn said, glad she wasn't stuck talking to a guy like Mitch.

"Are you going to tell us about the book guy?" Wanda asked.

Bitty crossed her arms. "Book Guy?"

Wanda pointed her finger at Evelyn. "Inside the bookstore, there was a very attractive man who knew Evelyn."

Evelyn wasn't about to explain her history with Charlie, no matter how quirky and good Wanda would be for her next story.

"I know him from way back, that's all," she said. "We worked together."

"At the bookstore?" Bitty asked.

It made sense, but she had met him waiting tables at that very spot. "We met on the island while working here at this restaurant. I'd come to work during the summers."

Every summer, while studying creative writing at Dartmouth, she went down to Martha's Vineyard and waited tables at The Wharf. She made enough money to pay for all the extra expenses, her food, and her dorm. Waiting tables for the ultra-rich gave her plenty of ideas to use in her books. The series she was most famous for had nothing but bits from working there. After she met Charlie that first summer, she would return to the island whenever she could. During the summer, they lived on the island, wrote together, dreamed together, got engaged—and almost lived happily ever after together.

"And now he owns a bookstore and you're an author?" Bitty must've found it amazing because she laughed at it all. "Wow, what are the odds?"

Evelyn almost confessed her feelings when she saw the bookstore's sign. It was like she had to go in, like something pulled or tugged at her to go into the store. Boy, were her instincts off. They were probably warning her to stay away.

"He was a bit of a jerk back in the day," she said, regretting it the minute it left her mouth, but what were two middle-aged women going to do with that information?

By the time they finished the margaritas, all three were ready for a nap.

"It's been a long day's travel," Wanda said, looking at her phone. "It says we can check in now."

Evelyn checked her phone. Still no messages.

"There are cocktails on the patio at six. Then dinner at eight." Wanda continued to read the itinerary out loud.

Evelyn had planned on attending nothing but her hotel room. She had a book to write. She had promised her agent as much. Thirty thousand by the end of the week. Five years ago, she'd finish that in her sleep. Now . . . she hadn't written more than a couple hundred for her Evelyn Rose books, here and there, for five years.

What was she going to do?

Give back the advance, for one. Put her tail between her legs and try to find another avenue. Maybe she should retire. Isn't that the next step?

She had nothing. No ideas. No plot. No characters or arcs. No feelings about how it should start or finish. She didn't even have a theme. She had absolutely nothing.

Well, she had margaritas and Wanda and Bitty. "Thanks for having lunch with me, ladies."

Wanda tapped her lips with her napkin, her lipstick dotting the linen. "It's better than talking about Mitch's revolver collection."

"Ooh-wee!" Bitty let out a holler as she slapped the table. "I believe we're going to be just fine on this trip."

CHAPTER 4

*W*hen they finished lunch, their rooms were ready for them. Evelyn followed them up to their rooms, and they all agreed to meet for cocktails before dinner. Wanda had a view of the water from her room, and Bitty's room had a fabulous bath. Evelyn stayed quiet about her luxury suite. She had upgraded thinking that's where she was going to stay put throughout this adventure, though now, she looked forward to drinks and dinner tonight.

She also wasn't tired like the other ladies and planned to write instead. She pulled out her laptop, made a cup of coffee, checked the headlines—twice—and stood on the balcony. Finally, after two attempts, she started. And like always, she stopped.

The persona of Evelyn Rose—the happily ever afters, the themes of love and inspiration—was gone. The stories in her head were hard, sad, and conflicting. Real, not fantasy romance. There were no happy endings in her stories now.

She slapped her laptop shut and gave up after a half hour of nothing real. She stared out the window, wishing, hoping, and praying something would spark inside her.

"He didn't have a single book in that whole bookstore?" She got up and picked up her phone. She called her assistant.

"Donna, if you receive an email with an attachment of a story, I'd like you to forward that to me."

"Funny you mention it, because I just got one." She could hear Donna click her mouse on the other end.

Evelyn had hired a personal assistant years ago. Donna had literally saved Evelyn's career. She did everything from Evelyn's taxes and appointments, grocery shopping and laundry, and everything else that needed to be done. She was also Evelyn's biggest cheerleader. She was lucky in that regard. She had people who worked for her who she considered friends. Her agent, Sue, had been a good friend. She encouraged her to work with the studios and helped her with the contracts and different investments she had made over the years. She helped find the right people that helped create her success. Not too many others had a career like hers, but she also had a duty to Donna and Sue and the rest of them. And they had no idea she hadn't been writing this whole time.

After George, she used old pieces from years ago and fixed them up—writing she had done on the side that she had no intentions of ever using. The series she handed over was a silly story of a mother and son living in a small town and the center of its gossip. She had no idea it'd get the attention that it did.

How did Charlie not have any of her books?

After letting Donna go, she opened her email and saw the name Harper on top. She opened the attachment and read the title, *The Mark of Nine*.

Dramatic, she thought. *Hmm.* She checked the vitals before reading. Eighty-seven thousand words—a lot for a newbie, but not for a fantasy like the title alluded to. Didn't Brandon Sanderson write like two hundred thousand or so? She scrolled through, seeing if there were glaring errors or mistakes, like red lines not edited out or just obvious amateur hour. She should've known that Charlie's daughter would be completely professional.

The story began with a prologue in a forest. The air was cold; the forest still and just at the beginning of dawn. A young lady is at the water's edge trying to escape something coming toward her. She's run out of time and strength. The epilogue ends, not letting the reader know if she survived.

Harper nailed it.

By the time she was supposed to meet the ladies for cocktails, she hadn't left the couch or manuscript. Harper's writing was certainly raw and in need of a very strong edit. She'd have to learn how to correctly punctuate, but the story was good. Really good. So good, she decided to skip drinks. Maybe even dinner. The ladies would be just fine without her.

When she heard a knock on the door, she wished she had texted them she had a headache.

"I'm coming!" She put her computer on the coffee table and rushed to the door.

"Here she is, Wanda!" Bitty exclaimed down the hall as Wanda came up to the door.

Both had showered and pampered for the occasion. Both looked at Evelyn with a half smile.

"I'm so sorry. I started doing some work and, well, lost track of time." She was about to come up with her headache excuse, when she stopped herself. She didn't want to come up with another excuse. Instead, she ushered them in. "I'll get cleaned up really quick."

"Take your time," Bitty said, stepping into the suite. "Oh, this is a lovely room."

The suite had a sitting area with two couches, a large window, and a deck that overlooked the water. The bedroom was on the side next to the small kitchenette. There was a sunken tub that sat up against a picture window overlooking the Vineyard Sound. It was a perfect room.

George would've loved it.

But she had never taken George to Martha's Vineyard, even when they lived on the East Coast. They did the whole New England thing, but never the island. She rarely talked about the Vineyard, and only recently did she start thinking about it. It started as one of those *what ever happened to the hotel and restaurant?* And then she Googled the island, looking through Google Maps to see what the tiny village looked like now. She had been a whole other woman back then. Not the wife; not the mother or the sister and daughter. She was carefree and excited about the possibilities she had at her fingertips.

She dialed room service and ordered a charcuterie while racing to the bathroom to clean up. "Feel free to answer the door when room service arrives."

She opened the mini fridge full of drinks.

"Girl, if you ordered cheese, I'm going nowhere!" Bitty called out from behind the counter with a chilled white wine from the fridge. She started opening drawers.

"Do you need something?" Evelyn asked, wondering if she'd be able to find what Bitty was looking for.

"Nope!" Bitty held up a wine opener. "Got it!

Evelyn looked to Wanda, who sat on her phone, browsing the itinerary, most definitely.

"I'm going to clean up," Evelyn said to her. "I'll be quick."

Wanda nodded and put a smile on, but Evelyn could tell something was bothering her. With the way Wanda was with the schedule, Evelyn had a feeling she didn't appreciate her running behind. Not that she blamed her. Evelyn usually liked timeliness. Back in the day, if she wasn't ten minutes early, she was late.

Now, time didn't matter much. She lived as if there were no time. One minute rolled into the next minute and then into the next. Before George died, time flew. Now it lulled and dragged and pulled.

She jumped into the shower, threw on a classic evening outfit she had worn occasionally years ago, and spritzed a few squirts of perfume on her hair.

As she walked back to the sitting room and saw Bitty and Wanda giggling over a plate of cheese, an idea popped into her head. She came into the room and immediately grabbed her notebook sitting on the coffee table next to her computer. She jotted a few words down to remember. It was only a seed, and it didn't exactly fit into the Evelyn Rose brand, and she might lose some readership, but of any other genre, she could make it work.

"How'd you hear about this singles' trip?" Wanda asked.

Bitty crossed her legs, stuffing her hand in between them. "One of my girlfriends bought the ticket for herself but ended up meeting Mr. Right right before. I'd never been to Martha's Vineyard, so I thought, what the heck."

"What do you think?" Evelyn loved seeing a first-timer.

Bitty smiled. "It sure beats my expectations."

"Were you married before?" Wanda asked.

Evelyn wondered the same thing, but she also didn't want to meddle in anyone's business.

"I was." Bitty laughed. "Three times."

"Three times!" Wanda's eyes opened wide.

Bitty grabbed her wineglass from the coffee table. "First one, I was too young and stupid, and I married my high school boyfriend. Second one broke my heart into pieces when I caught him sleeping with the babysitter. And my third husband . . . Well, my Richard was the love of my life." Bitty's eyes glistened, and she looked out the window. "Sure is beautiful hearing the waves all the time."

"I lost my husband five years ago." Evelyn sat on the other end of the couch next to Bitty. She hadn't planned on opening up, but suddenly, she didn't want to hold back. "I hate that now that it's been five years, people expect me to not care as much. It's like there's a time limit on grief."

"When Bill left," Wanda said, "I thought I was going to die—literally *die* from a broken heart."

Evelyn immediately thought of the heartbreak of losing Charlie. She didn't think she'd survive losing him. Loss was loss. Death was permanent, but to lose someone and watch them live on, to watch them live life without you . . . that must have been real pain.

"Do you really want to meet someone again?" Evelyn asked.

Both women looked at each other before Bitty said, "I would like to meet someone. Maybe just not on this trip."

"Do you think these people were vetted?" Wanda asked. She clearly wanted to meet someone.

"I'd do some research on the side." Evelyn hadn't signed herself up, but she was certain they weren't doing background checks.

"What kind of romances do you write?" Wanda asked.

Evelyn could switch into author Evelyn Rose like a light switch. "I write contemporary romance, small town."

She waited for the judgment. Even though the romance genre was a billion-dollar industry, throughout her career, she had been met with criticism from men and women alike. It killed her how many people pooh-pooed her stories as trashy, when honored fiction gave little hope, a scorned journey, and little change in character growth beyond the protagonist. Yet, her stories were about overcoming obstacles, finding true love, and being at peace with life's choices, but the critics considered it silly. She loved a shoot 'em up as much as the next guy, but why did violence trump love?

"Have you met Nora Roberts?" Wanda asked.

Evelyn nodded. "She's lovely."

"You'll find this one in the grocery store next to Nora." Bitty jabbed her thumb at Evelyn. "Are you writing something now?"

Evelyn was always writing; that had never been her problem. What she was writing was the problem. Getting past the first quarter was her problem. Starting over was her problem. Finishing anything was her problem. "I'm starting something this weekend."

"How many books have you published?" Bitty asked.

Evelyn took a second to go through her inventory. She had written dozens more unpublishable stories, but she didn't count them in her total any longer. Only books that someone else paid for and now owned. "Seventy-six."

"Seventy-six!" Wanda's eyes exploded open.

"I sure loved The Vineyard Series," Bitty said. "It's one of the reasons I agreed to come on this trip to the island."

"Aw, thank you." Evelyn needed to change the subject. She liked talking about writing with writers or people in the industry. But she didn't like compliments; they made her uncomfortable, even though her wretched self-confidence needed to hear them. "Should we head down soon?"

She picked up her shawl and placed it in her lap.

"We could just order some more of this wine and stay here on your deck?" Bitty said.

Evelyn liked that idea. "I bet the sunset is great up here."

"No, I think we should go to dinner." Wanda stood up, smoothing out her skirt.

Evelyn glanced at Bitty and gave a smile. "But one night we should have dinner, just us."

"Yes, another night," Wanda said, fluffing her hair, then pulling out her compact.

Bitty chuckled to herself. "Well, I say we all buy Mitch a drink." She winked at the ladies.

"We should." Evelyn laughed at the thought of Mitch receiving drinks from all three of them.

"Only if he's standing with another woman," Wanda said.

Bitty stood up. "That won't be difficult."

"It'll be like a warning to all the other ladies," Wanda said as they headed for the door.

Dinner was held under a white tent on the patio outside the hotel. Even though she had wanted to stay in her hotel room the whole time, she was glad she had gone out and made it to dinner. It was beautiful. Lights hung from the tent's ceiling, candles were placed around every table, the food was delicious, the sunset magical.

The three women sat together after dinner. A few other people joined them, men and women, but the three seemed to have made their pack.

"What's your type?" Bitty asked Wanda as they looked for Mitch.

"My ex always said I talked too much," Wanda said. "So, I'd either need someone who doesn't mind listening to me, or someone who likes to join in on the conversation."

Evelyn laughed at Wanda's standards. She hoped she wouldn't sell herself too short.

"Look." Bitty pointed to Mitch, who was standing with another woman from the tour.

It took fifteen minutes to send Mitch three different drinks from the three of them. They waved just as the waitress pointed to them at the table. He didn't seem to understand the humor, but the woman who stood next to him disappeared quickly after. All three went into a fit of giggles.

"One good deed done for the day," Bitty said.

As Evelyn laughed, she realized it was the first time she had *really* laughed in a *really* long time. When was the last time her stomach had ached with laughter?

"My makeup is going to get all ruined," Wanda said, wiping away tears.

Mitch avoided the three ladies for the rest of the night, but other men, some attractive, some not, from all over, came to talk to them. Wanda met a retired bank executive who retired in Provence.

"His name is Remy," she whispered in Evelyn's ear.

Evelyn talked and tried as best she could to mingle, but truth be told, she had no interest. She waited for the first opportunity to sneak out of the after-dinner drinks, but Bitty hooked her arm into hers and said, "Let's you and me grab a beer down at the tavern. By the beach. I saw there's live music tonight."

When was the last time she saw a live music concert? "You go see live music still?"

Bitty had to be in her sixties—but a healthy, fit sixty, not a beer-drinking, bar-girl sixty.

"I love music." She drawled out the word music like it was a song.

"I'm too old for music concerts," Evelyn said.

"Maybe an old stick in the mud, but no one's ever too old for music. Ask Dolly Parton." Bitty pointed her red manicured fingernail at Evelyn. "How many times will you be able to say you saw music on the water on Martha's Vineyard?"

Evelyn almost slipped with the truth, that she had gone to music on the water all the time during the summers as a kid, but stopped herself. Who was she kidding? Bitty was a stranger, not a soul sister. She was on vacation, and in less than a week's time, she'd be off on a plane back to Minnesota. She should go back to her room, lie in her bed, write, read, and scroll through Pinterest, not stay up and have a beer in a dank, dark, crowded bar.

But as Bitty squeezed her arm, Evelyn also didn't want to let her down. Yes, she may be a stranger, but there was a feeling of trust, something she couldn't describe. "Alright, I have a confession."

"Oh goody!" Bitty squeezed her arm even harder. "I love those."

They kept walking toward Harbor Lane.

"Well?" Bitty said. "You gonna tell me?"

Inhaling the tangy sea air, Evelyn paused briefly. Maybe it was the adrenaline kicking in after a *very* long day of travel and activities. Maybe it was the excitement of coming back to the island, seeing all the old sights and how little had changed. But everything was different.

"Do you mind if I take us on a little walk first?" she asked, feeling a bit brazen after her second cocktail.

She didn't want to walk all the way in the dark by herself, but a six-foot-tall woman locked arm in arm with her felt much safer.

Bitty didn't seem to mind missing the music. "And where are we walking to?"

"A bookstore."

"Ah, you want to spy on Book Guy," Bitty said.

"Charlie. His name is Charlie." Would he still be there? He had always been there when they were younger. He'd either be working at the hotel or reading in the corner of his aunt's bookstore. They had lived above, but he said he always felt more comfortable among the books in the store.

"Where is he from?"

"Here. He's an Islander."

"And what's the connection?" Bitty asked.

Bitty still had her arm hooked into Evelyn's. "We dated a bit when we were kids."

"This is going to be interesting," Bitty said. "When was the last time you saw each other?"

"Since we were in our twenties."

"And are you seeing if there's something still between you?" Bitty smiled. "Like your romances?"

Evelyn spun the meeting with Charlie around her head all day. Had he divorced Tanya or did she? Had he remarried? Did he even want to see her again?

Whatever the answer, Evelyn needed to know. Now.

CHAPTER 5

*C*harlie sat alone on a box in the back of the store, away from Harper and her endless questions he wasn't willing to answer and tried to collect himself. He pulled out his aunt's journal from the morning and opened its cover. Tonight, the writer's group was having a poetry reading for the high schoolers. The theme: Shakespeare. The crowd: dismal—the local high school English teacher, maybe a few students, their parents, and Harper.

His mind couldn't stop racing, thinking about the day. Thinking about Evelyn. She looked great, no doubt about it. Over the years, he had seen her in interviews on television or from a promotional photo when a new release came out. She had aged, which after over thirty years was to be expected, but she still looked as stunning as ever.

He ignored the bell as it hit against the glass. Harper could handle a crowd better than he could these days. His patience had slivered down over the years, and the rude behavior some tourists displayed got the best of him, but not his Harper. Nobody rattled his baby girl. Not even Evelyn Rose. He still couldn't believe she sent her manuscript.

He opened the first page of the journal. His aunt's writing had been cursive, and the script shaky at best. It was hard to decipher what the words even spelled, but that wasn't the only problem. Her writing was in a unique shorthand that only his aunt understood.

When he decided to rewrite it in a document, he had no idea he wouldn't be able to read any of it. He had hoped to preserve it for their family history, but he'd be lucky to get a few lines from the whole thing.

"Uh-hmm." Harper cleared her throat as she poked her head into the backroom. Then, in a loud whisper, hissed, "She's back."

"What?" He stood, wiping off any box dust that might have attached itself to his rear end. "She's back?"

This was unexpected. He never thought she'd step foot into the store again. Not after she hightailed out of there that morning. He still couldn't believe she was back on the island. but now Evelyn was back in his store?

He walked out front, and sure as the roses bloom in late spring, Evelyn stood in the back of the room where local parents listened as a student recited Nick Bottom's part in *Pyramus and Thisbe*.

"Shakespeare's always a classic," he said, approaching her. She stood next to a tall, slender woman, who he recognized from the singles tour group. She didn't seem at all surprised to see him like the last time.

"Hello, Charlie," Evelyn said.

Was Evelyn part of the singles tour group?

"Evelyn," Harper said in a sing-song voice, totally comfortable around a celebrity author. "I'm so glad you came."

Harper gestured toward the group of kids. "Please, join us."

"We can't stay long, but I wanted to tell you what I thought about your writing in person," Evelyn said.

Harper's hand went to her mouth. "You hated it."

Evelyn shook her head and let out her soft, sweet laugh. "Why would you think that?"

He had forgotten how beautiful it was—like the melody of a songbird.

"I loved it, actually." She pulled out her card. Her name donned the front, not her assistant's. "Just needs some fine tuning."

Harper appeared surprised, but not relieved like him. "It's okay, I can take criticism."

Evelyn shook her head, confused. "What? No. I really and truly loved it. You're just beginning, for goodness' sake. You have to learn by doing it, like any other career." She smiled at Harper, and Charlie flashed back in time. He never forgot how she smiled.

"You have the story down," Evelyn said to Harper—*his* Harper. His Evelyn was with his Harper. "And you have a very strong voice, and that's the hardest for most beginners."

"You seriously liked it?" Harper's jaw dropped.

Evelyn nodded as Harper squealed through her hands.

"I'd like to help you clean it up, and I can help with your query letter to find an agent."

"I can't believe this. Seriously?" Harper grabbed his hand and squeezed it.

"You're really good," Evelyn said.

Before Evelyn knew what she was doing, Harper ambushed her with her arms and hugged her.

Harper pointed at the kid who now wore a donkey head and called out over the crowd, "See, Jeremy, dreams do come true!"

The donkey made a hee-haw and quoted, "Methinks, mistress, you should have little reason for that, and yet, to say the truth, reason and love keep little company together nowadays."

The few in the crowd laughed, and Harper said, "I can't thank you enough for taking the time to read my story."

"And on her vacation," Charlie said, still grateful she offered in the first place. "That's really incredible. Thank you."

"I'm happy to help someone as talented as Harper."

He had known of his daughter's talent, but Harper, like her

father, was a stubborn beast who still wouldn't drink her milk or share a single piece of writing with him. Every time her teachers would explain her special talents, he'd ask to read it, but she'd never share.

He stood there staring as the two women talked.

"I really like the angle with the character Flora," Evelyn said. "And Flora and Michael are perfect together."

"Really?" Harper's eyes widened.

"And when the woman decided not to sell the book to Albert," Evelyn continued, "I loved how you made him fall back, and Eve was the one who got aggressive." She pointed to the card. "The first thing you need to do is get a query letter started. You can look it up if you don't know what I'm talking about."

Harper pulled out her phone and started taking down notes.

"Then let's get together and work on it," Evelyn said.

"That's really nice, but we don't want to disturb your vacation." Charlie couldn't believe her generosity, especially after the look she flashed at him that morning. Wasn't she still angry with him?

"You're not disturbing me at all." Evelyn smiled at Harper. "You have the gift."

"What's that?" Harper asked.

"You know how to bleed on the page."

She looked directly at him when she said it.

He almost apologized right there and then—almost fell on his knees and asked for forgiveness. He would if he thought it would work, but he'd just embarrass everyone there. He wished he could go back in time and fix things. Jesus, he would change so much.

The tall woman stood and clapped for the performers. "Bravo!"

The two performers bowed, and another teenager stood behind the microphone with a bass guitar and said, "My name is Owen, and I'm reciting Jimmy Hendrix's 'Purple Haze.'"

When Harper's attention had been stolen from one of the

parents, he stepped close to Evelyn. "Look, I've always wanted to tell you how sorry I am for all that happened between us," he whispered to Evelyn as Owen's speakers broke out in a screeching noise.

Evelyn shook her head. "It's water under the bridge."

People covered their ears with their hands as Owen recited each line from Hendrix's song.

"There's so much I wish I had said back then," he told her.

"It's not necessary." She shook her hands out, then tapped her friend on the shoulder. "We should go."

The woman didn't hesitate and hooked her arm in Evelyn's. "We're headed to hear some music down the street."

"Jimmy Hendrix isn't doing it for you?" Charlie joked, but he couldn't read Evelyn's reaction. "I'd love to catch up sometime before you leave."

"Yeah, sure," she said quickly, but she didn't leave her card with him. She didn't stay long enough for him to pass his information to her. She rushed out of his bookstore with her friend without looking back.

"She left?" Harper said, coming back from the stage.

He nodded, watching her and the friend head down the road.

"I can't believe it!" Harper's joy could be felt.

"It's great, Harp," he said, his gaze still lingering out the window.

"There's nothing I should know, right?" she asked, checking his expression. "Like, this isn't going to be some weird vendetta thing?"

"Are you serious?" He wasn't discussing his relationship with Evelyn with his daughter. "Evelyn is nothing but professional. She'll do what she said. You're extremely lucky. This could be big for you."

He tried to sound enthusiastic, but he couldn't find it for real. Why couldn't he be happy for his daughter? Why couldn't he be happy that this very private woman opened up enough for his daughter to catch a break? He should be over the moon.

"Do you still have feelings for her?" Harper asked.

"Don't be ridiculous, that was years ago." He waited for the guilt of lying to her, especially since he was certain she knew he was lying, but she walked away, bouncing around the store and cleaning up after open mic. It was a chore she loathed and complained about regularly, but tonight, she danced.

Then suddenly, with a finger thrown up in the air, Harper raced to the counter and started furiously writing something down. "I have a new idea!"

He felt cemented in place. How did he go from an ordinary day to one that could potentially change his life forever? One minute he's spilling coffee on his shirt and—boom!—he runs into the woman he had loved his whole life. Then the next minute, his daughter might be running toward a career that had chewed him up and spit him out.

What if Harper left the island?

Sure, she could write anywhere—but she could write *anywhere*. She wasn't married to the island. All she had was him now that Martha had passed, and for a young girl in her twenties, the island of luxury and tourism didn't offer much in the way of a singles' nightlife—unless you counted single dads at open mic night nine months out of the year.

No, once Harper earned enough to leave, he had a feeling she would take off.

Just like he had.

He had always wanted to write but mostly wanted to work in film or television, writing screenplays or scripts. He devoured the media, studied the craft. He took theater in high school despite the ridicule he received from the guys. He wanted to learn everything he could about the industry. But colleges liked football stars, not writing wonders, and an orphaned kid didn't have enough money to get in on his own.

He had been determined to get to Hollywood and applied to every local job, including The Wharf, the big moneymaker hotel that usually hired college kids for the summer to earn money.

"I heard you can cook?" the manager had asked at his interview. His aunt Martha must've slipped that in.

"I can." But he hadn't worked anywhere other than the little kitchen he shared with his aunt.

He wrote during the days as he worked at the bookstore, then worked at night at The Wharf. His life had turned upside down when he met Evelyn, the only other person in his life who wrote.

They'd written constantly together, and he had never written more in his life. They'd work and talk out their writing—their own critique group. They read everything together and discussed the author's craft and the book's themes and contradictions. They talked about planning and writing, developing characters, and creating tension. She loved motifs and he loved symbolism, which were terribly different, they'd agreed.

And then out of nowhere, a friend of a friend had set him up to meet Alex Murphy, a director who had just finished filming on the island. As a favor, Alex had read his screenplay, and the next thing he knew, Charlie was flying on a commercial flight to Los Angeles.

At first, they had tried to make the relationship work, but distance, time, and feelings got in the way. He was pretty sure she'd hated him when they finally ended things.

So much had happened during those years.

Did she still hate him?

Or, if she didn't, did she know he didn't carry her books?

"Earth to dad." Harper waved her hand in front of his face. "Please tell me you didn't break up with her."

He shook his head. "No, that was her idea."

"What happened?"

"How's Mateo?" he asked, knowing full well she'd understand.

She crossed her arms. "Well played, Father."

He nodded at his clever quip, then hit the lights. "I think we can handle the rest tomorrow morning."

It would be Sunday, and he didn't open until noon on Sundays. He'd have plenty of time to put the stage and chairs away and move the shelves of books and displays back into place. His space wasn't small, necessarily, but it was full, and full everywhere. The whole place was very big but tight with shelves upon shelves of books.

"When did you stop carrying her books?" Harper asked. She knew he had lied to Evelyn.

"I never have," he answered, slightly embarrassed now. He always had customers looking for the books; the series was set on the island, after all. It had done so well that it even had a television series.

He had found out about that when they filmed the pilot episode on the main strip in town, using the harbor and the ferry ride into the dock. They even had a shot of Martha's Mysteries in the beginning scene—the pan out of the heroine about to start her romantic adventure.

"Why not?"

He thought Harper was getting the hint, but apparently not. "That's none of your business, Harper." He walked to the alarm. "You ready?"

"Ouch." Harper's jaw dropped. "What's up with you?"

"What?" He typed in the code. The alarm began to beep, and they walked to the side door and out.

"How serious were you two?" she asked, prying even more.

"Harper."

"Like serious, serious?" Harper's eyes shot open. "What if she still loves you?"

He didn't know how much Tanya had told their daughter. Harper knew he had been with Evelyn, that they had been a couple, but did Harper know about the engagement, their separation, and his disaster of a response to it all?

"Believe me, she doesn't."

"What if you two are destined for each other?" Harper kept following him to his apartment.

She wasn't going to drop it.

"Let's play the quiet game."

She followed behind him as he walked up the back staircase to his apartment above the bookstore he and Harper had lived in since she was nine. Now that she had her own place, he felt as though she stuck around more now, which made him glad she felt comfortable enough to hang around with her old man.

"You should go to that thing they were talking about," Harper suggested. "The live music."

"Absolutely not."

"Come on, Dad." She slapped the counter for effect. "Moments of serendipity don't come every day. This is fate playing with you, giving you a second chance. Go see that music and buy a drink for the woman you still can't talk about."

"Good night, Harper." He opened the door to the apartment and stopped before entering. "You can come in, but I'm going to bed."

"You're being a donkey."

He didn't respond, because, well . . . she was right.

Harper kissed him on the cheek and took the hint and left.

He ended up not going to bed. Instead, he stared at the ceiling, thinking about this second shot. If anything, it was a second shot at apologizing. Eastport wasn't that big. He'd be able to find her if he looked hard enough. And what if—and this was a big what-if—Harper was right? Maybe this *was* a once in a lifetime opportunity, and he could settle their feelings after all these years. When things had ended between them, it was ugly, and he had always regretted how things had worked out.

It took a few calls, but when he reached the receptionist at The Wharf hotel, he wasn't surprised. She had the money to stay there.

"Hello?" Evelyn said as the call went through to the room.

"Evelyn?" he asked, though he knew it was her. "It's Charlie. I'm sorry I'm calling so late."

The other line stayed silent, which made him hear his heartbeat in his ears.

"I'm calling to ask if we could meet up for a coffee, or maybe lunch?"

"Coffee is good." Her voice sounded flat, and he wondered if she even wanted coffee or if she was being polite.

"I hoped we could talk." With another moment of silence, he decided to apologize right there on the phone. "I owe you an apology, and I was hoping to tell you in person how sorry I am for everything. I didn't handle any of it the right way, and I know I hurt you."

"Yes, well, it's all in the past." She snapped out the words, and a sting went through his heart, but he supposed he deserved it.

"Yes, and I'm sorry for that." He didn't say anything more, letting the silence hang between them. What more was there to say?

"Thank you," she said after a moment.

He wasn't sure if she was being sarcastic, but he responded with, "You're welcome."

He picked at the edging of his counter and scanned his apartment, wondering what Evelyn, bestselling author, would think. The bland and boring interior wouldn't impress anyone, he supposed. He suddenly wished he had taken more effort to decorate in his own style now that Martha had passed away. Knitted quilts and homemade needlework hung on the backs of the couches and chairs. It looked like an eighty-year-old woman lived there, not a bachelor in his fifties.

"Thank you for helping Harper. She's really excited," he said.

"Do you know how talented she is?"

He did. "Yes, her teachers always said she was creative." Harper would kill him, but Evelyn had to see the glaring problem with Harper's writing. "She always struggled in school, though, so she doesn't really understand the rules . . ."

Struggled is pushing it. She bombed. She almost failed out of school. She hated everything about it—the teachers, the schedule, the rules, the cliques. She started quoting Pink Floyd's "The Wall" in middle school, *Animal Farm* in high school, and wouldn't even think about college.

Charlie had almost lost it. How could his daughter not attend school? Even Martha couldn't get Harper to reconsider.

But there had always been something about her energy; her fire for life had made him anxious and content at the same time. He worried he wasn't doing what he was supposed to do as a father. Should he have been harder on her? Or easier? Being a single father was hard and isolating, and he'd had no other male friends that were raising a child by themselves; it was just women. And how horrible that society excused men but had shamed his own single mother.

He had been hailed as a saint at the school—Harper's teachers loved him—but it hadn't changed the fact that he was alone in this parenting gig, and alone in general. His mother had died when he was sixteen; his father had left town before that. Tanya still lived in Los Angeles.

"I'm actually finishing up her book as we speak. I made her some notes," she said.

He wasn't surprised. He remembered her voracity when it came to reading. She could devour Brontë in a night or Voltaire over the weekend. She'd daydream about what she read or predict what was to come. He admired that curiosity of the creative mind. She loved to dissect as much as to be entertained.

"Do you really think she has it?" he asked, not trusting his own opinion.

An author could only reach readers if their voice was unique, and what did the experts say about learning a craft, ten thousand hours? Did Harper need ten thousand hours? Or was she that special someone that came around once in a lifetime?

"She's got it."

His heart skipped a beat, and he let out the breath he had been holding. Then he thought of Harper's comment. Was she right? Could Evelyn still have feelings?

"Thank you."

"When were you thinking of coffee?" she asked.

"How about tomorrow?" His heart skipped a beat. "I have freshly ground coffee right here at the bookstore."

He didn't, but he could run across the street and buy some. Greg owed him one.

"How about tomorrow afternoon?" she asked, her voice light. "I'll come to the bookstore. I just talked to Harper, and we're going to meet."

"Really?" When did Harper talk to Evelyn? "Coffee sounds great."

He'd have to find someone to work for him, but he could ask Linda, who worked part-time, to cover a couple hours and close early. Traffic slowed down during the afternoons anyway.

"I'll see you then," she said.

"Yes, see you then," he said, but he was sure she had hung up.

If coffee worked out, that could lead to dinner. Maybe a walk along the pier or the beach like old times. Should he bring up the old times? Should he tell her that he still dreamt about her?

He called Harper. She didn't even say hello, just mumbled into the phone.

"I need help tomorrow afternoon," he said.

"Sure. But I have dinner plans." She didn't even let him finish.

"I need help with Evelyn."

Harper paused for a second, then said, "She's my dinner plans."

His heart sank. "You have dinner plans with Evelyn?"

"Yes. Would you like to come?"

Apparently, coffee meant coffee. Dang.

"Harper, there's something I should probably tell you before your dinner."

"What did you do?" she asked.

He took a deep breath. "We were engaged."

"What?!" She practically screamed into the phone. "You're telling me she could've been my mother?"

"She was never going to be your mother." He couldn't believe he was laying it all out there. What was he thinking telling his daughter this feely stuff? "Please, can we be done with this conversation?"

"Did she say yes?" she asked. "Why did you two break up?"

"Please be cool about this."

The phrase was one he had used throughout her childhood. Dropping her off at school, he'd say, "Be cool and stay at school." Her reaction had evolved over the years, from laughter, to eye rolls, to complete dismissal, back to eye rolls, then to sympathy. Now, he was pretty sure he was back to an eye roll.

"Dad, I'm always cool." Harper had been cool. She had to grow up fast when Tanya left them, and he had asked a lot of her for a kid.

"You're right." He had been the nervous, anxious parent who constantly worried about everything. He didn't want her to ride her bike outside their driveway. He had de-choking devices waiting in the wings just in case. He had practiced fire drills in the middle of the night. Learned how to perform CPR and more. "I'm having coffee with her tomorrow afternoon."

"Ohhh!" Her voice held a tone.

He groaned. "Be cool."

"Cool. Right." She sounded like she was eating something.

"She says you're a really good writer."

"Really?"

He could hear doubt but also pride in her voice. "I know how long you've worked on that story."

She may not share her writing with him, but she talked out her ideas with him—in the car, at the store, while they had break-fast at the apartment. She'd talk about the plot, and he'd remind her of the hero's journey. She'd talk about her characters, and he'd help her with their arc. She'd discuss the themes, and he'd keep her focused.

"You deserve this," he said to her.

It had been years of submitting and getting rejections. They kept telling her to get the college degree. He thought their intent was obvious, but she kept writing, one book after the other. She'd submit each one, only to receive the thin letter or standard rejection email, if she even got a response.

All of that had gotten her nowhere.

But *this* could be her big break. He just couldn't believe it was with Evelyn.

CHAPTER 6

That morning, Evelyn stood on the balcony at three twenty-three a.m. and stared up at the stars as the ocean waves lapped against the shore. The dark morning held a chill coming off the Atlantic waters. Mist rolled along the sand, and the musty aroma of campfire blended with the briny scent of the sea.

She had missed this place.

She took in a deep breath, inhaling through her nose like her yoga app instructed and then breathing out. She looked up at the moon. It wasn't full, but at least three-quarters. This was the time she felt most connected with George—just as the world woke up. Clouds swept by but didn't dull the glow of the light off the water. Was the moon waxing or waning? She could never remember which one was which. George would've. The stars seemed to go on and on as the water blended into the sky.

She waited for a sign, something from him. She swore she had felt his presence when she'd agreed to come on the trip, the pull she felt when she'd stuck around Wanda, and a ton of other things she'd felt after he passed. She didn't tell anyone, especially her family. She didn't want to be placed on medication, or worse, placed in a residential home for losing her mind. Who would believe George sent her signs? Maybe it was a figment of her imagination. Even still, she liked the idea that George was up there, watching over her.

Evelyn loved the mornings and always wrote best at that time. It was a habit she'd learned from her father. He cherished mornings and taught her to do so as well.

"Take advantage of the silence," he'd told her once as he sat in the dark at the kitchen table, watching the sun rise.

How she missed those days.

She wondered if the girls even thought about her. Two daughters and not one check-in. She had been gone for two days, across the country, and not one call or text or message. Nothing. It wasn't that she needed them to do so, but it seemed as though it didn't even cross their minds. And that was the problem. If she didn't nag, no one would notice she was around.

If she didn't invite the girls for the holidays, would they invite her to their celebrations? Her daughters lived their own lives, which was fine, but they didn't seem to have any time for her unless she was feeding them, paying for them, or doing something for them. She wouldn't call them spoiled necessarily, but they didn't seem to think beyond themselves at this point. She knew it was a phase. She had gone through it during her own twenties. Trying to find herself. Falling in love. Living life's adventures.

Now, Life was routine—three a.m. wake up, stargazing, write, write some more, and then write even more. She'd eat somewhere in between writing, thinking about what to write, and writing some more. She wrote and wrote and wrote but completed nothing. She created scenes but had no theme. She started an exposition but didn't have a conflict.

She was in trouble.

She didn't want to write the happily ever after with a man, but a woman's discovery of how to live without one.

The idea that a relationship could save her made the pain

worse. Especially now seeing Charlie. It was a love she never quite got over.

She sat down and opened her computer. After an hour of staring at a blinking cursor, she snapped the computer screen shut. Banging her head on the back of the suite's couch, she suddenly remembered the journal she had bought at the bookstore. She got up, rushing to the drawer she had stuffed it in, and pulled out the leather-bound book. She brought the cover to her nose and inhaled its musky scent. She loved a brand-new journal, the fresh, crisp pages and the endless possibilities of what she could do with it. Lists, reflections, musings, poetry, art, nothing—the list went on and on.

She had written in a journal since her tenth birthday. The diary had been a gift from her mother. A white-and-purple hardcover journal with a lock. She wrote that night and almost every night after that until she became an adult. Sometimes she'd write a sentence or a word. Sometimes she wrote pages upon pages. When life was good, she spent more time writing. She'd be more creative with what she wrote, more observant. When life became overwhelming, she wrote very little—quotes, lists, words.

She opened the cover and pressed down on the spine, breaking the seal of the binding. She liked to be rough with her journals. She liked them used, bent, torn, dirtied. She stuffed papers, receipts, tickets, bills, postcards, fortunes, dirt, and anything else from the moment of life inside them.

She turned to the second page, leaving the first blank. Later, she'd figure out a quote for the time period; for now, however, she would start with the date on the second page.

She wrote it out in cursive, though she had to grab her reading glasses in order to see the lines. She wrote out the day, the month, and the year in words.

With her favorite pen in hand, she wrote the word *Journey* smack dab in the center.

As she stared at the word, a warm sensation flowed throughout her body like a wave washing up the shore—a peace she hadn't felt in a long time. And that's when she saw the sun flitter over the horizon. Rays twinkled up from the other side of the earth, and the clouds above were bright pinks, and magentas, and oranges, and white dots floating in the wind. A seagull glided above the clouds, high in the sky. She stood up and walked to the balcony, opened the door, and stepped out. Her eyes moistened as the feeling grew and the seagull came closer, almost calling to her.

"Oh, how I miss you," she whispered, her bottom lip trembling. She tried to hold back her emotions. She didn't want to start her morning this way. Her hand wiped away the tear that fell, and when she looked up, a gray-and-white feather floated in front of her. She reached out and caught it in her hand.

She looked up to the sky, and the seagull floated in the breeze above her.

She watched as the bird swooped down toward the water, practically skimming the surface with its underbelly. It was a beautiful flight.

A knock on the door jumped her out of her bird-watching trance. She remembered her promise to take Wanda and Bitty to go for an early morning walk up to the Gray Head cliffs.

"Yoo-hoo," Wanda called out.

"You up?" Bitty said after.

She rushed to the door and swung it open. "Good morning."

Wanda and Bitty stood at the door, ready for the walk in their yoga pants and running sneakers. Wanda's wild red curls were stuffed under her visor but escaped from the top. The curls gave her height, though her petite frame only reached Bitty's chest. Bitty had her short hairstyle blown out and her makeup already applied. Her fancy tracksuit sparkled and dazzled as they stood there in the hall.

"You girls look like we're hitting the town, not taking a walk," Evelyn said.

"Can I use the restroom before we go?" Wanda asked.

"Yes, of course." Evelyn pointed down the hall.

Wanda scooted down the hall, and Bitty went to the sliding glass doors that open to the balcony.

"This must be a perfect spot to imagine your stories," Bitty said. "Do you come to Martha's Vineyard often?"

Evelyn shook her head. "I haven't been back since I was in my twenties."

It felt so long, but yet, as she looked out at the view, everything felt familiar.

"What made you come now?" Bitty asked. "And on a singles' trip, when it looks like you have some unfinished business with Book Guy?"

Unfinished business, she thought to herself. Was it unfinished or has it been done, and was she picking at old wounds? Looking into things, making it harder on herself for no reason.

"I'm not sure," she said honestly. "I guess I'm here to write my next chapter."

As cheesy as the analogy had been when her sister Carol had used it against her, it was exactly how she felt. This stage in her life, these past five years, she had been stagnant, and stagnant anything created disease and deterioration. She had been doing the same thing over and over, day after day, for five years, waiting for an outcome that she knew would never come. There was no doubt in her mind she would eventually deteriorate.

"I always found refuge here on the island." She wasn't surprised Carol had found the trip back to her beloved Martha's Vineyard. She wrote an entire book series on it, had a television series set on it, made a career using its natural beauty as the backdrop of America's romances. Her little sister wasn't thinking about Charlie. She probably thought Charlie was still in Los Angeles with Tanya. But Evelyn knew. Evelyn knew Charlie had moved back. She knew going to the island meant she'd most likely run into him. The bookstore was the first place she went. She may not have realized it until now, but Bitty was right. "But yes, I guess we do have some unfinished business."

They didn't stay long in her suite after Wanda used the

restroom. They headed toward Sugar Beach, where there were walking paths along the coast and marshes. It was her idea to take a walk, knowing about the pathway from when she lived there in the summers. She took them along the water and showed them the red brick lighthouse up on the Vineyard Hills.

They continued along the water's edge, Bitty looking for sea glass. Wanda stopped and rested every once in a while, saying she was still exhausted from all the traveling. Luckily, Martha's Vineyard's coast didn't disappoint. The soft beige sand glowed under the summer morning sun's rays as sanderlings raced against the incoming waves. Seals sunbathed on the granite boulders in front of the lighthouse. Nature's beauty at every turn.

"Gorgeous." Bitty took a picture of the sunrise again.

She pointed to the different landmarks on the Vineyard Sound. "This is called Sugar Beach and is a conservation trust protected beach. And over there is the Elizabeth Islands."

She pointed out to the water, past the lighthouse.

They walked along the packed sand, the three of them side by side. Evelyn took them on the wooden staircase up the cliffs all the way to the end of the beach, where the salt water reached the cream-colored clay cliffs. The seagrass swayed in the wind like individual ballerinas dancing in synchronicity.

"Ooh-wee, that is a lot of stairs, but worth it for the view," Bitty said once they reached the top.

They stood looking out at the Atlantic Ocean. Waves slapped against the cliffs. She inhaled the tangy salt air and exhaled and with it so did some of her anxiety.

"Sure is pretty." Wanda pulled down the sides of her visor. She found a bench and took a seat.

"I've always wanted to live in one of those houses in the hills," Evelyn said, pointing to what the locals called the Vineyard Hills. Like the ocean waves of the Vineyard Sound, the hills and valleys of sand dunes and seagrass rose and fell with sea cottages sprinkled throughout. Each house connected to the beach with wooden walkways and staircases.

The hills offered a one-of-a-kind view of the island and cliffs. Small footpaths traveled throughout, twisting and turning through the cliffs and coves, but always leading them to the water. As a young adult with no money, she had dreamed of one day coming back and living on the island. Buying one of the cottages. Living and writing by the water in a place of refuge, escaping the trouble of life.

"That one's for sale." Wanda pointed to an old Victorian gambrel clapboard house just a few walkways away.

"I wonder how much a place like that would cost?" Bitty asked, starting to follow the wooden plank walkway, and then down another toward the house.

Evelyn hesitated. "That's private property."

"Do you think a sixty-year-old, gray-haired woman is a threat?" Bitty asked. "Besides, it looks empty."

"But what if it's not?" Evelyn didn't like the idea of tramping down someone's personal walkway to their private home, but at the same time, she was curious. Nestled within the hills, the gambrel clapboard had a terrific location overlooking Sugar Beach. She didn't know much about architecture, but the house was at least half a century old; she guessed even more. A house like that would most likely be bought up and torn down, which made her a little sad. She loved the old clapboard fishermen houses.

"Now that's a price tag!" Bitty whistled as she read the real estate agent's information about the house.

Evelyn looked at the details. It was high, but not a bad price. Then she noticed the listing date. It had been on the market a hundred and eighty-six days. The blurry photographs didn't hide the fact that the four-bedroom house had a lot of work that needed to be done. Yet the price, along with its unbeatable view, was worth it, even if the place had to be demolished. Why wasn't someone scooping this amazing property up?

"I can only imagine what the sunrise is like at this spot,"

Evelyn said, turning to face the water, imagining all the changes the cliffs would go through throughout the day.

"Oh, look at the cute stone fireplace." Wanda pointed in the window.

Evelyn peeked inside and saw a tumbled stone fireplace with built-in bookshelves on either side. Two leather chairs were set up to face both the fire and the view, but the room was mostly empty.

She continued to meander down the porch, peeking in the windows and stopping at the sliding glass door. With her hands pressed against the glass, she peeked inside. The interior looked like a traditional boxy New England floor plan. Too bad because there was a lot of potential with all the woodwork and beams throughout.

Just as she was about to walk away, she looked down to see a white-and-gray feather at the foot of the door. Bending down, she picked it up, twirling it in her fingers.

"Be careful," Bitty warned her. "Birds carry diseases,"

But she continued to twirl the feather in her fingers. Was this a sign? Was George leading her to this house?

She peeked inside the door's window again. The house had the typical middle staircase cutting it down the middle. The kitchen was on one side, leaving a large living space on the other. She walked along the porch that wrapped around the whole downstairs to the other end, where there was a small but decent-looking bathroom with more linoleum than she had seen since the seventies. It was dark inside, but with a few renovations and some doors removed and walls taken down, it could be bright and airy. She stretched to peek through another window, pulling out her phone and taking pictures of the inside, then a shot from the window of the ocean view. A sensation swept over her—one she hadn't felt in a very long time.

She was in love.

"Should we head back for breakfast?" Bitty asked.

Wanda began to head down the walkway toward the beach's trail.

Evelyn lagged, staying on the deck, and typed in the number of the agent who was listed. "Just give me a minute, and I'll catch up!"

She waved Bitty and Wanda to take off without her. When they reached the beach, she could see Bitty stopping every few feet to pick up pieces of sea glass.

She pressed call and listened as the phone rang. On the fourth ring, a voicemail of a woman picked up. "Hi, you've reached Lisa Ryland. Unfortunately, I'm unavailable, but if you could leave your name, a number, and a brief message, I will get back to you as soon as possible."

Evelyn took in a long inhale. *Okay, George, I'm ready for my next adventure.*

"Good morning, my name is Evelyn Rose, and I'm interested in your listing."

CHAPTER 7

*A*t breakfast, Bitty told stories of growing up on a cattle ranch, riding horses and taking in stray cats and dogs. Wanda talked about growing up in the suburbs of Pittsburgh, working for her father's furniture store business. Her ex-husband had been her father's top salesman.

"Bill could sell a waterbed without water," Wanda said.

The conversation flowed, and Evelyn was part of it, but her mind was on the beach house for sale. When her phone began to ring, she jumped up and answered it right away, immediately leaving the women at the table. She walked out of the restaurant and into the hotel's lobby, away from the large echo and different groups of people.

"Ms. Rose?" the agent asked on the other line.

"Yes, this is Evelyn Rose," she said, her voice gaining a business-like seriousness. George had always dealt with the serious stuff in their lives, like buying the cars and taking care of the mortgage and loans for the girls' college. He talked to the auto mechanics and anyone who came to the house to fix appliances. He dealt with everything. Could she buy a house on her own?

"Yes, this is Lisa Ryland. You called about my listing on Vineyard Haven?"

Her heartbeat raced inside her chest. Was she really doing this? "Yes, is it still available?"

"It's funny you just called about the property. A buyer just pulled his offer yesterday out of the blue," Lisa said over the phone. "It looks like serendipity is playing a role in your new dream home."

Maybe the real estate agent meant it for real, or most likely it was pure coincidence, but she couldn't help but wonder if it really had been serendipity having a hand in things. The feather that morning, the feather at the door, and the buyer pulling his offer.

"Would you like to see the property? I could meet you right now." The agent knew she had her.

And she did. Evelyn looked at her watch, then glanced back at the ladies at breakfast. "I can meet you in a half hour."

She'd have to walk. She didn't have a car and doubted the buses for tourists went through residential neighborhoods.

She walked back into the dining room where Wanda and Bitty sat waiting for her return.

"Everything okay?" Bitty asked.

She almost kept it to herself. Was she crazy? But then she realized that these perfect strangers were the perfect people to confess her secret to. "I think I'm going to buy that beach house."

Wanda covered her mouth with her hand.

Bitty dropped her silverware against her plate. "You're kidding me."

Evelyn let out a laugh, looking at the recent call on her phone. "I have to go. I'm going to meet up with the agent in a half hour."

"Let us go with you." Wanda put her napkin on the table and took a sip of her water. "You should have another set of eyes."

"She's right," Bitty said, putting her coffee down and grabbing her handbag. She threw a hundred smack dab in the middle of the table. "This one's on me, Girls."

"But—"

"But nothing." Bitty pushed her chair out. "Let's go see the inside of your beach house."

"It's not mine," Evelyn said back. This was crazy. Buying a beach house on Martha's Vineyard was crazy. "Plus, I don't have a car, and you're already tired from the walk earlier," Evelyn said. "Stay. I'm being completely ridiculous."

"I've got Uber!" Wanda held up her phone to prove it. "I downloaded the app before I left and it works." She pointed to her phone's screen. "Look at that. I just press this and tell them where I am, and where I want to go. Where are we going?"

"22 Cliffside Point," Evelyn quickly answered.

"It's going to be here in . . . ten minutes." Wanda looked triumphant, as if getting an Uber had been the journey.

"I've got to go to the bathroom." Evelyn laughed, rushing to the ladies' room.

The three women paraded off to the restroom, gabbing the whole way as if they had been dear friends forever. They filled the restroom with laughter and shrieks of excitement. They couldn't contain it. Evelyn might be buying the beach house in the hills.

"Does it have one of those names?" Bitty asked.

She hadn't noticed any name. "I don't think so."

"You have to come up with something romantic, yet whimsical." Wanda continued talking as they waited for the Uber. "Serenity by the Sea or maybe Cliff House."

It took five minutes to get to the house. She hadn't seen it from the road's perspective, but she was more in love every second that passed by.

"It's adorable," Wanda said, looking out the window.

"It's like a Thomas Kinkade," Bitty agreed.

She had to admit the outside of the house looked like something out of a magazine. The closer they got, she could see the gray clapboard and white trim needed work. The window boxes now had weeds growing, along with a couple pine tree saplings. The porch steps had patchwork fixes that looked unsafe. The whole place needed a lot of TLC, but there was no question in her mind. She wanted it.

The real estate agent got out of her Mercedes-Benz; her license plate read SOLD. The house had three stories if you included the dormered attic, along with a porch that wrapped around the whole house. It sat in a valley of sea grass and dunes. The houses around were spaced out, giving the property a lot of privacy.

"Welcome to your beautiful vacation home," Lisa said, holding out her hands. "This is an incredible piece of property."

The real estate agent began talking about the location but didn't really mention anything about the house—funny how the gambrel-style house was what drew Evelyn in. The house, with its decorative molding and rounded dormers and gray clapboard, felt warm and welcoming. It sat protected from the cold Atlantic winds, nestled in the valley of the hills. The home seemed to call to her.

She walked up to the front porch, taking in the view as much as she could, videotaping the whole experience so she could go back with a neutral eye later. Right now, her emotions and excitement made her feel as though she were stepping back in time to when things were simple again.

The panoramic view was like no other. The cliffs jutted out from a white sandy beach on the other end, only a few hundred yards away through a wooden plank walking path. In the very distance, from the back deck, she could make out the tip of the lighthouse on Gray Head. At night, she'd be able to see its beam of light most likely.

Lisa jammed the key into the keyhole and twisted, forcing her shoulder into the wooden frame. "It just needs a jiggle."

She shook the key, and finally, the door popped open. She stepped back and held out her arm, welcoming Evelyn inside. "Please come in and look around. I'll be right outside waiting if you ladies have any questions."

"This is marvelous," Bitty said, walking down the wooden floors.

The wood floors creaked beneath Evelyn. In the back was the kitchen and family room. The front had two rooms that had been made into guest rooms. All the rooms were small and cumbersome. The kitchen hadn't been updated since the eighties, with mauve-colored linoleum countertops and linoleum faux tiles for the floor. The whole house had pine paneling throughout, with shell décor displayed on tabletops, shelves, and counters. The upstairs had four bedrooms and that included a master and full bath. The third floor was one large space with three sets of bunk beds.

All in all, it was a dump. The bathrooms were overused and under-cleaned. All the appliances were on their last leg. Everything was sticky and sandy and smelly. The floors didn't feel level. The basement looked disastrous. What if there was a hurricane or any kind of storm? Maybe she would be risking her life by living in it.

"Am I crazy if I love it?" She looked at Wanda, then to Bitty.

"Absolutely crazy," Wanda said immediately. "But I love it too."

"Me too!" Bitty said, squeezing her arm. "It's just perfect if you ask me."

"I see the kitchen here." She pointed to the wall that separated the kitchen from the dining room. "And I see a wall of doors that open up."

"Here too." Bitty swung her arms on the other side of the room.

"Yes, there too." Evelyn had never been one to gush over interiors. She didn't care if her walls were gray or light gray or gooseneck gray, but something about the house radiated inside of her. She had to have it.

"Get it," Bitty said. "If you can afford this place, get it."

Evelyn walked around, looking at the cabinets, pulling out all the drawers. She peeked inside the closets, noting the lack of storage, and the garage wasn't attached. Where would she park in the winter? Could she even get here in the winter? Would this be only a summerhouse? What if there was a storm? Did she board up? Could she physically do the work that this house required?

She walked up the staircase. The boards didn't just creak; they moaned and cried out. No one could sneak around this house. The roof line slanted in the bedrooms, and a double closet didn't signify a master bedroom in her mind, but it did have a full bath. She'd rather make one of the downstairs bedrooms into a master. Maybe she could add on.

"Is this crazy?" she said as she came back into the kitchen.

"What a dream for yourself," Bitty said, leaning against the counter.

"So, you think I should?" Evelyn didn't know.

"It's about having faith in yourself." Wanda spoke so quietly that Evelyn almost didn't hear her. "Making the right decision for *you* and not anyone else. I wish I could do it."

"I thought you loved your little community." Evelyn remembered how much she talked about the community she was from on the boat ride in.

"All they talk about is death," she said. "I don't even look when I see an ambulance anymore because they come by so frequently. When a new neighbor moves in, the group swarms them like animals, and worse when a spouse dies." She looked at them. "All I wanted for this trip was to meet someone who likes adventures, a friend I could talk to, watch movies and read books with. I had high hopes, I guess."

"The trip isn't over yet," Evelyn reminded her. "This morning, I had no idea I'd be buying a beach house, but here we are."

"Well, this is a gem. What are you going to do?" Bitty asked, sitting next to Wanda at the round table. The table sat next to a set of sliding glass doors.

Evelyn opened one and stepped out onto the porch. The back's vista overlooked hills of seagrass with wooden plank walkways and sandy paths leading to the water, tethering the houses to the ocean.

The sunlight glowed off the water like millions of diamonds as seagulls cried out above her. The faint sounds of waves crashing into the cliffs could be heard off in the distance, even though the beach in front of the house appeared calm. She focused on the water—so blue it blended with the sky on the horizon. Off in the distance, a sailboat with its sails billowing in the wind chased a feather-shaped cloud in the sky.

"You better know what you're doing," Evelyn said to the cloud. She turned back to Bitty and Wanda, and said, "I'm going to make an offer."

"Hot dang!" Bitty clapped her hands together, and Wanda let out a giggle.

"This is so exciting." Wanda placed her hand on her chest. "I can't believe it."

It took less than a half hour to make the initial offer. All she had to do now was wait. The three of them decided on skipping lunch and doing a bit of window shopping for some new decorations for the beach house.

"You should look at local art," Wanda suggested.

"That's a great idea." Her mind spun wildly out of control. Did she just make an offer on a house on Martha's Vineyard? "Is this absolutely nuts?" she asked again for the hundredth time as they stopped in front of a gift shop.

"Yes," Wanda kept answering, but this time, she playfully elbowed her. "I'm a bit jealous of your ability to just go for it."

"Usually, I have to plan, organize, and plan some more." Evelyn didn't usually write her novels by the seat of her pants. She plotted out each chapter, practically writing the book out with all her planning, but then when it came to writing, all she had to do was type. It was as if something came over her.

It was George who was the irrational one. If there was a sale on anything, God help her. He'd come home with televisions, a car. One time, he even bought a boat because it was a good deal. He would've been the one who bought this beach house.

Her phone buzzed with a text, and she immediately looked. It was from Charlie. **Looking forward to coffee**. She had almost forgotten about coffee. Almost.

"Is that from Bookstore Romeo?" Bitty asked.

"Have you seen him again?" Wanda asked.

Evelyn glanced down the road in the direction of Martha's Mysteries. "I'm having coffee with him this afternoon."

She also wanted to finish Harper's manuscript. When was the last time she felt out of time?

"You're getting your money's worth with this trip," Wanda said, and all three laughed together.

Evelyn didn't know if she had just made the biggest mistake of her life or finally started living again, but an energy pulsed through her body, a feeling that made her lungs expand with every breath. The weights of burden, of death, of rot, disappearing. The sun was finally shining, and she wanted to grab it and take hold.

"I need to get ready," she said suddenly.

"You should buy that pretty sundress in the window over in the shop." Bitty pointed to a soft-blue linen dress that hung on a mannequin. "It'd go perfect with your blue eyes."

The feeling radiated, and she realized she hadn't had true friendships like this in a very long time. After George died, most of their couple friends were uncomfortable inviting her without him. They included her at first, but the invitations came less throughout the year, eventually waning to hardly ever. Would anyone even notice if she left the suburb she and George had lived in for the past twenty years?

Would she sell the house? Would the girls want it?

They still hadn't called.

She nodded. "I think you're right. I should buy a new dress."

After trying it on, and twirling in front of the girls, Evelyn purchased the dress, and all three walked back to the hotel.

"You better tell us everything," Bitty said as they parted in the elevator.

"I will." Evelyn squeezed her hands together, trying to hold in the anxiety and excitement and everything else running through her body.

When Evelyn returned to her suite, there was a message on her phone.

"Congratulations, Ms. Rose. They accepted your offer!"

CHAPTER 8

"*I* bought a beach house," Evelyn said to Charlie the second she sat down with him at coffee.

"You did what?" He shared her shock as his eyes widened. "Here on the island?"

She nodded. She still couldn't believe it. "Yes. I saw a place near Gray Head and called the real estate agent this morning, and bam! Now I own a beach house. Like own. With a key."

She threw down the brass key on the table between their chairs.

The bookstore had a cute and quaint set up. Two high wing-back chairs sat in front of a picture window looking out at Harbor Lane, where small shops lined the cobblestone road. The ferry that traveled the tourists back and forth to the mainland came every hour with a new group piling off and piling on. Bicyclists, small mopeds, and walkers filled the narrow street.

"Tell me everything," he said, handing over an iced coffee she had ordered when she came into the bookstore. She had gone straight to the counter and ordered. She could tell he wanted to do it himself, but she would buy her own coffee at this point. Besides, it helped with her anxiety, which grew by the second. She equally dreaded and anticipated this coffee meeting.

"I took a walk up to Gray Head, along the beach," she began. "And I saw this adorable Victorian for sale."

"The Buckley's place. Wait, you hiked that this morning?" He looked more surprised about her hike than her purchase. "I just finished walking it with Stan."

He pointed to a dog that lay on the floor by the counter. Stan looked like he didn't do much walking, or anything for that matter. She hadn't noticed Stan before, but the overweight bulldog was charming in his Red Sox jersey. "Still love the Sox?"

"Always."

She jabbed her thumb behind her at the dog whose belly protruded higher than its head. "Was he here yesterday?"

"He's getting older, so I only bring him on days that are slower."

She looked around the store, hoping to see Harper. "Is your daughter working today?"

He shook his head. "She's out buying an outfit for tonight."

She looked down at her own newly purchased dress. "I can't believe I bought a house."

"You own it, own it?"

The transaction had gone so quickly, but large cash down payments make purchasing a beach house much easier.

"Well, not until it's worked out with the banks, but they'll let me start renting it right away."

The road had been *the exact* spot she'd often walk or ride her bike, dreaming of someday living on the island with . . . She looked at Charlie, who studied her. "What is it?"

"Thanks for meeting me for coffee," he said, picking at his mug with his thumbnail. "I wish we did this sooner."

She wouldn't have met with him sooner. She questioned meeting with him now. If it hadn't been serendipity stepping in, if her sister hadn't pushed her to go on this trip, if she hadn't had Wanda, she wouldn't have had the nerve to find him. She had no intention of seeing him while visiting. Sure, it was a small island, but it had thousands of tourists visiting its little piece of land each day. She hadn't been ready.

George, she mumbled in her head.

"If we're being honest . . ." She *really* did want a fresh start. She did. This is the moment—a new house, a new location, new friends. But nothing would change if she didn't let go of the past. "I'm glad too."

She sipped her coffee and peeked out the window. On the other side of the street, she saw Bitty and Wanda poking their heads over a clothing rack in the gift shop. She laughed to herself as she thought of the last twenty-four hours.

"Would you have ever believed you and I would be sitting and having coffee after all this time?"

"I'd wish it," he said.

She could feel an almost whiplash by his honesty, and she remembered how strange it felt. Her family had been very prim and proper, Midwesterners through and through. Don't talk about feelings or any uncomfortable topic ever, and pretend nothing's wrong. Honesty wasn't the best policy if it made someone feel something.

And she was feeling so much right now.

"You wished to see me again?" She had wished it too, in distant daydreams, like one did after an argument. The reliving of an imaginary alternative to the truth, where she got the upper hand or said exactly what she meant at the right time.

"I wished I could have apologized so many times," he said. He let out a long sigh, and she could feel the air around her shift. "I'm really sorry for everything."

"We were kids," she said as an uncomfortable feeling she didn't want to feel again lingered in her stomach.

"I'm really sorry," he said again, catching her eye.

Ugh, she felt it, and it made her mad. "Look, I'm not here to relive it. I'm here to have coffee and small talk and let bygones be bygones and go on our merry way."

She took the utensils around her and started tidying up on the table, ready to dash off at any second.

He didn't say anything.

She shook her head, tears glistening in her eyes. What was going on with her? Why was she crying? It happened thirty years ago. How did she get here so fast? She drew in a long breath and counted to four, then released through her mouth, slowly regaining her composure.

"Evelyn." The way he said her name was like hearing a song from years ago but remembering all the notes. "I'm really sorry to hear about your husband."

"Yes, well, thanks for that." She wiped her eyes, embarrassed by her emotion and dug for the strength to get through without breaking down.

Charlie reached across the table, placing his hand on her arm. "I heard he was a great man."

She wiped her hand on her leg. "Yes, he was."

"How did you two meet?"

She could feel her head resist further conversation, but her heart remembered the easy feeling Charlie gave her while he listened, as if what she had to say was the most important thing in the world. And before she could stop herself, she began to tell her ex-fiancé the story of how she fell in love with her husband.

She was surprised when two hours had passed, and they were still talking. They talked about everything. They talked about when she met George and how they settled down in a small suburb of the Twin Cities. How her parents passed away after long battles of diseases. She talked about her girls and how quickly they grew up. But she didn't talk about the last five years.

"I wish I had listened to you," he confessed.

She knew he referred to their last fight, their very last moment as a couple. She had warned him about the greasy Hollywood executives. Charlie's confidence let him settle, let the smoke and mirrors of Hollywood cloud his judgment.

Charlie knew he had a gift in writing. Yet, he lacked the confidence to believe in himself as much as Evelyn had. She knew he didn't need to sell his manuscript for a cheesy network that would butcher the plot, kill the theme, and commercialize the heck out of it. By the time the show started, it no longer resembled much of Charlie's original novel.

And it bombed.

Charlie's brilliance had been dulled and distorted. No one got to see the real writer.

"They own the rights for another five years."

"Ugh, I'm so sorry," she said. She had heard these stories for years. Authors give away their work to be published or produced in a different media but get buried under millions of other projects never to see the light of day. Evelyn knew she was lucky. Her family had provided a safety to be patient to wait for what she wanted. "Have you tried buying back your rights?"

"It's out of my price range, I'm afraid."

He played with his mug, which was empty, rolling it around on the table. "I regret a lot of things."

He told her how Hollywood had chewed him up and spit him out. How Tanya stuck around, but had been miserable with him.

"She left when Harper was seven," he said. "And then Martha offered me the bookstore and apartment."

"You raised Harper all by yourself?" Evelyn asked, surprised.

"Don't look so shocked," he said back with a chuckle.

She raised her hands in defense. "No, I knew you'd be a great dad. It's just, you left Hollywood and came back here with Harper, but without Tanya?"

He nodded. "If it wasn't for my aunt, I don't know what I would've done."

She had liked his aunt. Very much actually, now that she thought about her time at their apartment above the bookstore. But she couldn't believe Tanya just let her daughter go.

"Did I ever tell you about the treasure map?" Charlie asked.

She shook her head. "A treasure map?"

She could feel his excitement as he told her the story of the island's legendary buried treasure. She suddenly remembered how much she loved when he told her his tales. She remembered so many wonderful nights next to a fire, the ocean lapping behind them as he told her stories.

"My great-great-great-something or other once saw a pirate ship anchored offshore by Gray Head. Supposedly, he noticed a few of the pirates rowing to shore. He snuck up on the cliffs and spied as they came to shore and buried what he believed was a treasure chest."

When he went back home, he wrote everything he could remember about the location and went back the next day when the pirates were gone, but he never found it. He died going mad trying to find it."

She thought about the cliffs. "Have you looked for it?"

"Only when I was a kid." He studied her again. "What if I told you I found my great-something -or-other-uncle's map?"

"You did?"

He looked around the bookstore. Besides the mid-thirties woman behind the counter, they were alone. "I found Martha's old journals, and one has a map of Gray Head."

"Really?" She couldn't believe it. His very own treasure hunt. "Do you really think there's treasure?"

He shrugged. "I guess I'll have to go look for it. It is documented that pirates used the inlets as a place to hide loot. Not too many people would go wandering into these dark, granite caves."

He held up his finger and said, "Hold on."

He ran off to the back room and came back with a journal in his hand. "It's Martha's."

She didn't take it, shaking her hands at him. "No, I couldn't read someone else's journal."

Something like that was so sacred to her.

"Let me show you, then." He flipped to a page of a drawn-out map. It was almost childlike, like something one would see in a children's book, but there was a square where her new home sat drawn right on the page.

"That's my beach house." She pointed to the square shape drawn along the shoreline, in the section titled Cliffside Point. She looked for the typical *X marks the spot* but didn't see anything. "Where's it buried?"

He pointed to the cliffs. "I don't know."

She looked again at the map, confused. "I thought this was a treasure map."

"It's a map of all the different locations mentioned in her stories about the treasure map."

She noticed several markings throughout the map, over a dozen or so. "I do love a treasure hunt."

"I started typing out her journal, getting everything on a document in the cloud."

"You should write a story about it." She thought about his book she had read at least a dozen times. At least. She hoped he couldn't read her thoughts and looked around the room. "This place is nice. You've made it quaint and welcoming."

"You've been a great success," he said. "I'm happy for you."

"So happy, you don't even carry my books?"

There it was. She could feel the truth hit him. He may have been happy, but something kept him from carrying the work of one of the big five publishers' top authors. She knew her worth, and it was on a middle shelf, front and center.

He looked down into his mug. "The truth is, I never could get over you."

She looked up at him, shocked. Her heart pounded inside her chest. "What?"

He placed his mug on the table and looked into her eyes. "I know you didn't buy a house on Martha's Vineyard for me, but I sure hope we can be, at the very least, neighbors."

She honestly hadn't thought about being neighbors with Charlie. What was she thinking? Could she only be neighbors with him? At this point, she wasn't sure if he was part enemy or the love that got away.

"I can't . . ." She spread out her fingers, focusing on the tension in her tendons. "Tell Harper I look forward to dinner." She stood up. "Thanks for coffee."

And left.

CHAPTER 9

A lot had happened, but a lot was the same, and it complicated things. Even his ritual afternoon coffee had been disturbed, and now his evening walk.

"Come on, Stan, let's turn back." He thought about skipping his walk, that way he could avoid her. But instead, he walked straight up to the property. The Buckleys had owned the house for as long as he could remember. A family from Westborough, outside Boston. They had kids, then grandkids, and then great grandkids. Not one of them wanted to keep their family's little piece of heaven on earth.

He walked up to the back slider and peered in. Stan sat on the deck, glad to take a rest. The inside looked rough—cheap carpeting and flooring, laminate everywhere in the kitchen. Nineteen eighties screamed out from the fluorescent bulb fixtures in the kitchen. It would be a lot of work.

A lot of work.

She had the money, no doubt. He wasn't lying about her career. He had been happy for her success. She deserved it. Evelyn had always done the hard work, put in the long hours, and did everything she needed to do to create a successful writing career. She was at the top of her game. He wished he could book someone like her. He would have a crowd, no doubt, especially all the middle-aged women who loved her romances.

He didn't carry her books because it was too painful. Because he loved her. Because reading her stories about her idea of love killed him silently. He gave up the best thing in his life to have the worst thing—Tanya.

He did get Harper out of the marriage, which had been the gold lining, but he'd accepted long ago that he'd never really get over Evelyn. Those summers with Evelyn had been amazing; every minute they spent together. He had never felt like that about anyone. He had never fallen so hard.

He took her to this very beach countless times, walked this very spot with her, passed this dang beach house with her.

He looked in, thinking about walking with her along the beach. Her hand in his, strolling along without a care in the world. Had he known what he knew now, would he change things? He looked out at the cliffs. Ducks floated off in the water. The cove's sand was bright from the sun, but the shadows were too dark to see inside.

"What's the plan, Evelyn?" he said to the house. Was she escaping from it all? Was she retiring and finally using the fruits of her labor? Or was there a piece of her who came to visit the past?

That summer had been everything to him. He fell in love, finished his very first manuscript, and had been riding high on the endless possibilities his future held. Then, like a Shakespearean tragedy, everything fell apart.

And now, he was middle-aged, alone, with a grown daughter who had a life of her own, maybe even a new career of her own, and he was stalking his ex by peeking into her new house. He was pathetic.

The way she had walked out at coffee reminded him of the time he first met her.

She had stormed into his life like a nor'easter. No warning, no time to prepare.

~

That summer, she came to the island following her boyfriend. A prep school, Ivy League type that had a summer house on the island. A house with acreage and a pool beside the ocean.

When she first arrived at The Wharf, he joined in with the guys, admiring the new beauty. Her blond curls and bright blue eyes were striking and bewitching. But then she spoke. She used vocabulary like the guests, upper class and uptight.

"Where you from?" someone asked her.

"I'm from Dartmouth."

"You mean Hanover?" he snidely said.

"Yes, I guess that's right."

She guessed?

The next few weeks, he seemed to be stuck with the princess from Dartmouth, who was a total snob and much too aloof to have a conversation with a line cook. After their shifts, the crew would usually get together at someone's place and hang out or go to the beach and have a bonfire. She'd never attend. Her boyfriend would drive up in his fancy two-door sports car and pick her up, taking her to much more fabulous outings on Martha's Vineyard.

Then one day, he saw her sitting alone on the shore, writing in a notebook.

"I thought I was the only one who wrote here," he said, holding up his own journal in his hand. He usually didn't confess that he wrote. The guys gave him a hard time about it.

She didn't even look up, her eyes covered in sunglasses. "I can move."

She started to get up, and when he went to stop her, he noticed she had been crying.

"Are you okay?' he asked.

She feigned a smile, but tears fell down her cheeks. "I'm fine."

She picked up her notebook and pen and stuffed them into her bag, rushing off.

"Hey! I didn't mean to make you leave," he called out after her. He stood for a second, watching her take off, but something inside him couldn't let her walk away, no matter how he felt about her. "Are you going to be okay?"

"I'm fine," she said back at him.

"You don't look fine."

"I just need to get off this godforsaken island." She stopped walking and faced the water. "I'm just waiting for the ferry."

"You're leaving?" he asked.

"As soon as I can." She wiped away a runaway tear.

He could feel her pain, physically *feel* it. He'd never been one to feel others emotions, but Evelyn's was palpable. He wasn't going to let her leave—not alone, not this upset and vulnerable.

"First of all, I can't let anyone speak about the love of my life like that."

"Who?" Her forehead wrinkled in confusion.

"The island." He flung his arms out at the water. "This place can be a refuge for the lost and broken. It's like the ocean. You can toss in something breakable"—he crouched down to pick up a piece of aqua sea glass—"and it becomes something beautiful. All you need to do is open up to it."

He placed the smooth, dull-edged piece of glass into her palm. She closed her hand, holding it, focusing on the water. "What's the second thing?"

"The second thing?" He didn't know what she referred to.

"You said first, so there must be a second."

"You're leaving us in a lurch."

"What?"

"You accepted the gig at The Wharf, and if you skip out, then one of us has to cover your shifts and ours. That's not cool."

"People aren't cool. That's what I've learned on Martha's Vineyard." She wiped another tear away. "I just want to get away."

"From him?"

She didn't flinch, didn't defend the penny loafer wearer. Her gaze was on the horizon. She inhaled, closing her eyes, a lone tear falling down her cheek, clinging to her chin. He reached out with the back of his hand and wiped it away.

For a long moment, all that could be heard was the waves crashing into the cliffs beyond them.

Then she asked, "What do you write?"

He pulled out his notebook—a small pad—from his back pocket. "Junk mostly."

He wrote everything from spy thrillers to poetry to mysteries, but now, he was writing the next great American novel, or at least he hoped it would be. A tale as old as time—a regular man finding his way through a society that didn't accept him, and it revealed its ugly truths and injustices along the way.

"People think I write junk too." Her tone was defeated, her pain raw.

"You have to be somewhat good to be at Dartmouth." He assumed someone who came from Dartmouth would think his writing was silly. He had no fancy degrees, no fancy professors teaching him the craft. Just a bookstore and a crazy aunt who believed she came from a bloodline of pirates.

She looked hurt and shook her head. "I don't think I'm going to be able to go back to Hanover."

He caught her correction and felt bad he had given her a hard time. "Don't tell me it's because of loafer guy?"

How did guys like him get girls like her in the first place? Then treat them so badly and get away with it?

She looked out at the water again. "No, because I write junk."

"Prove it," he said.

"Excuse me?" The look on her face let him know that she thought he was crazy, but he didn't care.

"Let's see it." He pointed to her notebook.

She shook her head. "I can't just hand over my notebook and get judged on it."

"Why not?" He shrugged, passing his notebook to her. The little spiral had been in his pocket for weeks. It was tattered and falling apart, folded in half and swollen from salt water.

She took his notebook and plopped down there in the sand, opening its blue cover that had a faded-out eraser mark from one corner to the other diagonally. She flipped through the pages. Most of his scribblings were notes, bullet points, details he didn't want to forget, quotes he wanted to reread, advice, observations, or the day's events. His notebooks were his ramblings—thoughts flowing from his subconscious.

She kept flipping, saying nothing, and all that hot air that he blew now turned ice cold. His confidence drained with each silent turn of a page. He had an impulse to snatch it back out of her hands, but he looked away instead, watching the cliffs and thinking about what he needed to do next.

"But you're not a wanderer," she said. She tapped her finger at the page of bullet points with his book idea for *Into the Great*. The main character was a wanderer and went on adventure after adventure. "Right?"

"Huh?"

"You should write from the perspective of the settler. The one who didn't go for it. The one who sat behind watching everyone else,"

Did she see right through him? He just stared at her.

"I feel like the character's journey would be more relatable," she added. "Yes, you want to go along on the adventure with the character that's brave enough to do it, but you feel more connected with the character that's scared and is put to the test to challenge themself to do it."

He could literally feel himself falling in love with her right then and there.

"There are apartments above the kitchen at The Wharf, and a lot of the staff rent a room from them." He didn't know what he was doing, but all he knew was that he wanted her to stay on Martha's Vineyard. "You could talk to the kitchen manager, Sal, about it."

She didn't say anything, just closed his notebook and passed it back to him.

"Where else are you going to go?"

"Okay." She wrapped her arms around her knees, facing the ocean. "I'll give Martha another chance."

He stood up and held out his hand to her. She hesitated, then took it.

After that, he spent every day with her. They worked together, they wrote together, they spent their free time together. They were inseparable.

∼

"Charlie?" a voice said behind him.

He didn't need to turn around to know it belonged to Evelyn.

He felt like a snake being there at her new beach house, spying on her. He turned to face her. "I'm sorry. I should've asked permission to be here. I'll leave." He held up his hands in surrender. "I'll leave right now."

"Dad?" Harper walked up behind Evelyn.

He felt like an idiot at this point. Like a stalker or a creepy guy sneaking around.

"I'm really sorry. I thought you'd be out to dinner. I've always wanted to check this place out, and well, I—" He shot Harper a look, flashing help signals, but no one stopped his ramblings. "I know this really looks bad, but I didn't think you would be here and . . ."

"Would you like to see inside?" Evelyn asked. "I was just about to show Harper as well."

"I don't want to intrude."

"I'm inviting you," Evelyn said, pushing her key into the keyhole, then twisting to the left. "You're not intruding."

Maybe this was a truce. Maybe this was her way of saying things didn't matter anymore. Maybe this was her way of saying he never really made a difference to her. Maybe she was trying to be just neighbors. God, he hoped not.

It was a bluff. He wasn't sure if he could be neighbors with

Evelyn. Could he have a casual relationship with the woman he had loved for most of his life? He looked out at her as Harper walked inside.

"I should head back," he said, jabbing his thumb behind him. "Sorry, again, for trespassing. You have a great spot here."

"I heard if I open up my heart, it could be a refuge for the lost and broken."

He froze and locked eyes with her. Time may heal, but her feelings hadn't changed for him. She wasn't changing her mind about things. Just like she hadn't years ago.

She left him, and she wasn't coming back.

"Good luck, Evelyn."

CHAPTER 10

"My dad told me you were friends with my mom," Harper said after Charlie took off. "It's weird to think you probably know more about my mom than I do."

Evelyn nodded in agreement, but uncomfortable about the subject. It felt weird. She saw no resemblance of Tanya in Harper. Just Charlie's dark brown eyes and auburn hair.

"We had been good friends." Evelyn wondered how much Charlie had told Harper about all of their connections.

She continued to listen as Harper talked about world building, but her thoughts would trail off about Charlie and Tanya's marriage and how it must've fallen apart as soon as it started. She remembered Charlie reaching out a few times after everything, but it was over for her. She wanted nothing to do with him.

Now, with the decades of time making things clearer, she realized she had missed an opportunity. She wouldn't have changed anything, because it had all led to George, but she wished she had been more open to resolving things.

Over dinner, they had talked about writing, about ideas, and dreams. Evelyn gave her pointers about making a pitch and building a brand. Harper told her about new authors and podcasts.

"You know, I'm really glad I met you," Evelyn said to Harper, which made the twenty-something beam. "You're right at the beginning of a very big adventure."

Evelyn knew her writing had it. There were few people who held the gift like Harper and Charlie. Evelyn didn't. Even after publishing seventy-six books, she still didn't have it. With all the fanciest schools, and the top-quality teachers, and the private tutors, Evelyn had never learned the real secrets to writing a powerful novel.

You had to believe in your instinct when writing. Evelyn worried about what everyone thought—would this upset someone, was she pushing the reader away, did she offend someone by saying that? She wanted clean, comfortable, and calm.

"Your father was the one who taught me how to write while listening to my gut and—"

"Feeling your heart," Harper interrupted. "My dad uses that piece of advice all the time. He'll say, 'You know, that's how Evelyn Rose got to be who she is.'" Harper eyed her from the side, her left eyebrow raised. "He told me that he's never been able to get over you."

"Excuse me?" Evelyn said quickly, but she had heard Harper. She bought time because what did she say to the daughter of a guy she had loved so long ago?

Harper shook her head. "Sorry. He's going to kill me, but I just think it's fate. You're back and buying this house, and he's here and like . . ." She stopped. "He told me not to say anything—well, begged me actually—but I don't care. I can't hold my tongue. I can't be cool. This is like every novel you've ever written. You're literally living a Hallmark movie. You have to see this, right?"

Harper's voice had increased with every second. Evelyn loved the young woman's spirit, but there was a lot of history tied into this. "It's really not that easy."

"I am sorry about your husband," Harper said.

"Thank you." Evelyn looked down at her napkin in her lap.

George was still a topic she couldn't just whimsically bring up, especially with a stranger.

"I don't know what exactly happened between you and my dad," Harper said. The twenty-something didn't seem unabashed about digging into Evelyn's personal life, which was equally nervy and impressive. "But I haven't seen my dad like this ever. Not even when my parents were together."

"I thought we were here to talk about a book?" Evelyn really didn't want to talk about Charlie with his and Tanya's daughter.

"I know this might cost me, but I just can't sit and watch my dad so sorrowful, so deeply conflicted, about the past."

Conflicted? How about guilt? Or regretful? Or remorseful? "Harper, you're really lovely, and I've enjoyed my time with you, but I'm not here to talk to you about your father."

"Then why come to the island?" she asked.

"Because it's Martha's Vineyard," she said back, as though it could be that simple. But were Harper's questions getting to her because she was crossing the line or talking truth?

"You must've known it would stir up memories of those days."

It did. Undoubtedly. It was why she changed her mind a hundred times before going on the trip.

"Maybe you're here to heal?" Harper leaned forward, practically resting her whole body on the table to get as close to Evelyn as possible. "He's read every one of your books."

Her heart stopped for a second. He read her books? But wouldn't carry them in his store?

Evelyn called it a night quickly after that. She promised Harper to finish the novel and to attend another writer's group.

The rest of the night, Evelyn kept thinking about Charlie reading her books. The look on his face when she saw him at the house, and how fast he took off when she invited him in. She wondered if he had noticed the connections to their past life in her books. Had he remembered some of the events, names of places, or music being played at the exact spots and at the right time?

The next morning, Wanda and Bitty met Evelyn at her suite and went for their walk along the beach to Evelyn's new beach house.

They stood in the living room as the morning sun streaked in through the dusty air.

"I can't believe you bought it," Wanda said, her mouth still agape from the news.

"I think it's so cool." Bitty walked the perimeter of the bottom floor. Evelyn had already called a contractor the night before, from Harper's recommendation. It was a local man that Harper had gone to high school with who owned a construction company with his brothers.

Evelyn couldn't help but smile as she stood there, looking at the dark, dank house. The whole thing was ludicrous. She had planned to call her daughters last night and tell them, but she worried they'd think she was crazy and try to change her mind, and she didn't want to change her mind.

Yesterday had been the first day in so long that she had been really *living* and not just hoping to get through the day. She could inhale and breathe. She could feel her energy flowing through her body. She felt ecstatic at the possibilities, a pride she hadn't felt . . . ever. She had followed her dreams and worked hard to accomplish this. The fact she could pay in cash was because of *her* hard work, *her* sweat and tears.

She deserved this.

"Thank you for not thinking I'm absolutely crazy," she said.

"You're my hero." Bitty clapped her hands together. "I get to live vicariously through you."

Evelyn didn't feel like a hero. Instead, she wobbled back and forth between insane and brilliant, but something else had happened last night.

She wrote.

She felt the magical enchantment that only writing could bring her. Last night, she began another story. But this one felt different because it felt like before, when writing had transformed her. When writing let her escape and dream and hope.

Last night, she felt like Evelyn again.

And it felt new.

And good.

And she was happy.

"What are you going to do first with the house?" Wanda asked.

Evelyn glanced around the room that hadn't been updated since the last time she stepped on the island. "Everything."

"I love your idea of opening up the space," Bitty said from the galley kitchen that had hardly any natural light. "It really doesn't take advantage of the views."

"There's a lot of work that needs to be done." Wanda crossed her arms against her chest. "You should hire one of those interior design companies."

Evelyn had already thought of that. "I got a couple names from a friend."

Harper had turned out to be lovely, as she'd suspected, and even with her inquisition, Evelyn adored Charlie's daughter, and the more embarrassed she felt about her behavior with Charlie. She didn't mean to be so abrupt and dash out of the bookstore like she had, but she would've lost it right then and there. Her emotions had been out of control these past few days. She should go back and apologize, especially after he took off last night.

"Evelyn?" Bitty waved her hand at her. Evelyn shook out of her thoughts and stood back at the house. "Where'd you go?"

"Sorry," Evelyn said. "I was thinking about dinner last night with Harper. How was the dinner cruise?"

Wanda sat down at the kitchen table. "It was lovely."

"Mitch was there," Bitty said.

"Oh boy." Evelyn waited for the Mitch story.

"He actually danced with four different women." Wanda shook her head.

"You seemed mighty fine with Remy last night," Bitty said. "I was up in my room by nine, and this one didn't get back until midnight."

Evelyn swung her head to Wanda, who sat blushing at the table. "The banker from Provence?"

Wanda squeezed her knees together with her hands on top. "We took a walk along the water. I even showed him your house. You girls must think I'm silly to keep trying."

Evelyn could see the sparkle in her new friend's eyes. "I think it's wonderful."

"I haven't willingly stayed up to midnight in so long," Wanda said. "And of course, I'm up at the same time. My body cannot sleep past six."

Evelyn hadn't slept more than a couple hours each night since George died, but last night was different. When Charlie left the beach house, it bothered her more than she could understand, and she hadn't slept a wink.

"How was your dinner?" Bitty asked, as if reading Evelyn's mind.

"Strange, but nice." It was the best answer she could come up with, but the women waited for more. "My mind is racing with everything."

"Are you having second thoughts about the house?" Wanda asked.

"Yes," she said truthfully. "But it's being back on this island and seeing Charlie and helping his daughter and it's all happening so fast."

"I knew it!" Bitty clapped her hands together. "You're having a second chance romance."

Evelyn shook her head wildly. "Oh, no. No romance. Just memories and reminiscing, that's all."

She was about to change the subject, but she stopped herself. These women had no judgment. Why was she holding back?

"His daughter says he's still in love with me," Evelyn blurted out, looking away before they reacted.

"I knew it." Bitty slapped the table.

Wanda's mouth dropped. "Do you feel anything?"

She shook her head. "No, I mean, of course I feel something. This is a man I almost married."

She joined them at the table. She didn't talk much about the marriage that didn't happen. Even with George. Certainly not why it didn't work out.

"What happened between you two?" Wanda asked.

"We just grew apart." Evelyn gave the easiest answer.

"Just grew apart?" Bitty raised an eyebrow, suspicious. "Seems like a lot of chemistry after all this time to just grow apart." She looked directly at Evelyn. "I know failed relationships, and the electricity between you two didn't sizzle out, that's for sure."

Had Evelyn ever been really honest about her feelings? "He hurt me more than I had ever been hurt before, and well, I don't know if I can get over it even now."

She paused, waiting for Bitty or Wanda to give their two cents, because she could hear it now. So much time had passed. Things have changed since then. They've both gone through a lot.

"Life's too short to hold on to past pain," Wanda said. "Forgive him for yourself. Then go from there."

The advice was so simple, yet she hadn't thought of forgiveness for herself. What did she have to forgive anyway? She was happy to have met George. She wouldn't change a thing.

She looked to Wanda, about to say something, when she noticed the cold sweat on Wanda's forehead. "Wanda?"

Wanda took hold of the table's edge, her face pale, and she looked like she was about to get sick.

"Wanda, are you alright?" Evelyn rushed to her side.

Bitty grabbed hold of Wanda's petite frame. "Tell us what's happening."

"I think I need to go to the hospital," Wanda said, leaning into Bitty, but her eyes were on Evelyn. She looked scared.

CHAPTER 11

*M*artha's Vineyard Hospital was comparatively small to other hospitals Evelyn had been to, but the staff were helpful and professional. She and Bitty sat in the waiting room with other families.

Even with a husband as a doctor, Evelyn never got used to the smell of a hospital.

"Do you miss being a nurse?" Evelyn asked.

Bitty had told her about her career as a traveling nurse as they sat next to each other.

"I miss the people," Bitty said. "But not the swollen ankles after my twelve-hour shift."

"My husband was a doctor." Evelyn loved the fact George had been a doctor. A career he loved and lived for. His practice closed for a whole week to mourn his loss. Hundreds came to his funeral.

"What did he specialize in?" Bitty asked, holding her purse in her lap.

"Pediatrics," she said. George had been good with kids. So good, in fact, she would question her own mothering to his fathering. She was even a little jealous sometimes, since he had been the one who knew what to do all the time, even in crisis.

On the other hand, she had been the nurturer of the two. The one who got up in the middle of the night to help with sickness, scary dreams, or when they were unable to sleep. She packed their lunches until they graduated, went to every game and recital for both him and her. She volunteered as troop leader for Girl Scouts, was treasurer of the PTO, and brought more gluten-free, organic cupcakes than any other parent in her daughters' classrooms throughout the years.

She was proud they had grown up strong and independent, because she didn't want them to grow up like her—someone who fell apart when she was alone.

Five years had been the longest she'd ever been without someone in her life since she was in high school. Her therapist had pointed it out when she first started attending her sessions.

"You have jumped from one relationship to the next without much breathing room," she'd said to Evelyn. She stopped going after that.

Right after Charlie left for Hollywood, she met George in Boston. He had started his residency at Boston General Hospital after finishing at Harvard Medical School. She was finishing up her Master of Fine Arts in Creative Writing at Emerson.

"I sure hope she's okay," Bitty said, looking back to the hallway where they had wheeled away Wanda.

Evelyn had been praying the whole way to the hospital, as Wanda looked worse and worse.

"Ms. Rose and Ms. Lightfoot?"

Evelyn stood up right away, rushing to the nurse. "Yes, that's us."

The nurse's face looked solemn and serious. As she approached them, Bitty asked, "How's our girl doing?"

"I'm afraid she's going to be admitted and transferred to Boston." The nurse's eyes flickered back and forth from Bitty to Evelyn.

Evelyn's heart dropped. "Can we go and see her?"

The nurse nodded and pointed to a set of doors. "She's in room 112."

"Is she going to be okay?" Evelyn asked.

"I'm afraid I can't answer any more questions, but she'll be leaving within the hour." The nurse looked down at a file and called another name.

They rushed down the hall, passing small rooms filled with patients on each side of the hallway. Wanda's room was at the very end.

Bitty knocked softly as Evelyn peeked inside the room. "Hello?"

Wanda lay on the bed, her eyes closed, an IV hooked up to her arm and machines going. Two nurses stood beside her as they walked in.

"Are we okay to be here?" Evelyn asked one of the nurses.

The nurse beside her bed nodded and moved aside. "Wanda, looks like you have some visitors."

She gave them a nod as if to say they were okay to approach her.

"Hey, Wanda. You gave us quite a scare," Bitty said. She pulled a chair up to the side of the bed.

Wanda's eyes opened slowly, and she gave a faint smile. "You came?"

"Of course." Bitty looked at Evelyn, who smiled back at Wanda.

"We don't know what's on the schedule without you," Evelyn joked.

Wanda smiled and closed her eyes again. "I fear I had a bit too many activities for my old soul."

"You're younger than me," Bitty said jovially.

But the energy that usually buzzed out of Evelyn's friend was now replaced with a heavy cloud of sickness.

"What's going on?" Evelyn didn't want to pry into her business, but it had been frightening. By the time the ambulance came, Wanda had been almost unresponsive and confused.

"I have urinary tract infection," Wanda said, quietly.

"Well, that's not the end of the world." Evelyn felt relieved. But Wanda still seemed upset.

"The UTI is the least of my problems ..." Wanda said, drifting off. A tear fell from her eyes. "I booked this trip when I found out my cancer came back."

"Oh, Wanda." Bitty leaned to Wanda's hand and took hold of it. "You'll get through this."

Evelyn's heart dropped. "I'm so sorry." She walked around the other side of the bed and took Wanda's other hand in hers. "What can we do to help?"

"There's nothing to do." Tears fell in a steady stream down Wanda's face. Her eyes stayed closed. "I didn't want to die alone. I wanted someone there for me."

"Who can we call?" Evelyn asked. She knew the community had to have someone who knew Wanda well enough. Maybe they would know how to get in touch with her family.

Wanda shook her head, her eyes still shut. "I don't have anyone to call."

A burn in the back of Evelyn's throat stung her eyes. She knew what loneliness felt like. Evelyn looked through her tears and saw Wanda's spark had ceased, replaced with acceptance.

"Listen, Boston has some of the best care there is," Evelyn said from experience. "My husband worked at Mass General. You can't find a better place to heal. Let me call a friend who I know."

"Thank you." Wanda closed her eyes again. "But they told me I could take a medical flight back to Palm Springs."

"You could stay with me." The words came out of Evelyn's mouth before she could stop them. "Then come to the city for treatment."

Bitty rested her hand on her waist. "Aw, y'all are going to be roomies when I have to head back to Oklahoma?"

"Stay with us at the beach house," Evelyn said impulsively, but nothing sounded like a better idea. Why not have them stay? She hadn't felt such a connection with others in years. Never in her wildest dreams would she have thought of having a roommate again, much less two, but she didn't want Wanda to go through cancer alone. How could she go back to her beach house knowing Wanda was going back to an empty house to a retirement community watching ambulances drive by? No, Wanda deserved ocean sunrises and soft sand between her toes.

"Please, I shouldn't have said anything." Wanda wiped her eyes with her hand. "I'll be fine. I've always been fine."

Bitty made a face. "You might need help. I've worked with patients who are undergoing treatment. It's a lot on your own."

"Stay and we can help with appointments and cooking and cleaning." Evelyn was determined to have Wanda stay.

"What about your own families?" Wanda asked. "We only just met. You just bought the house."

"That's big and empty." Evelyn hadn't really thought about how big and empty until now. "Stay and enjoy the summer at least. The three of us will have such a good time together."

Bitty laughed. "Staying on the beach on Martha's Vineyard instead of dealing with the Oklahoma heat? Sounds good to me."

"You have children," Wanda said.

"My son is a grown man with his own family and responsibilities. He doesn't need his momma around much anymore." Bitty pulled out her phone. "In fact, I'd love to spend time with y'all."

Evelyn's heart lifted in her chest. An excitement grew along with it. "Come on, Wanda. Stay. Let us help you." Evelyn patted her leg. "We met for a reason."

"I thought it was to snag a sugar daddy?" Bitty joked.

Wanda opened her eyes again, tears welling up. "I don't want to be a burden."

"You wouldn't be a burden." Evelyn laughed at the idea of living with these women. "We're all on a new journey—together."

Doubts quickly crossed her mind as she stood there, hearing the machines, seeing all the tubes hooked up to Wanda. Evelyn had never been in the face of illness before, only broken bones and minor surgeries. Cancer was a whole different beast. And selfishly, what would happen if the worst came? Stage three wasn't a walk in the park. Would she be okay if she went through with caring for Wanda?

"He left the first time I was diagnosed," Wanda whispered. "He had been having affairs for years, but we had started counseling."

"That's horrible," Bitty said, still holding her hand.

Evelyn took her other hand in hers. "We can make sure you get the best care."

"Please, I'll be fine," she cried, but she leaned into Evelyn's arms. Her shoulders shook, and Evelyn could feel nothing but skin and bones.

"We'll make sure of it," Evelyn said as she rubbed Wanda's back.

The truth was, Evelyn wasn't sure what she was doing, but maybe she came to help heal not just herself but Wanda too.

"We'll meet you in Boston," she said, taking charge. "Is there anyone you want us to call?"

"No, I'll contact those that need to know on my own." Wanda caught her breath and said, "This is too much for you."

"Nonsense," Bitty said. "Do you really think God sent all of us to Martha's Vineyard to meet Mitch?"

Wanda smiled but wiped her eyes. Closing them again, Wanda let go of Evelyn's embrace and lay back on the bed.

"Thank you." She fell asleep before they were able to reciprocate.

The nurses ushered them out, and they left the emergency room.

Evelyn had gotten used to the Uber app. "I have a ride coming in fifteen."

"It's an incredible offer. Are you sure?" Bitty asked.

Doubt may have swept through in the heat of the moment, but the more she thought about it, the more she wanted to do this.

"I've never had to take care of someone with this kind of illness, but I'm willing to help any way possible."

Bitty patted her on the arm. "You're a good soul."

Evelyn didn't know what came over her, but she reached out and hugged Bitty. "I'm so glad I met you."

Bitty squeezed her back. "You have no idea."

When they released each other, Evelyn opened the home screen on her phone. "I think we're going to need some transportation besides Uber." She searched for rental cars. "Let's get something fun to drive her back and forth to Boston."

"That's a great idea," Bitty said.

"Then some decent furniture," Evelyn said, hooking her arm into Bitty's.

"You know what's in Boston?" Bitty asked. "Lots of amazing shopping there on Boylston Street."

"Are you sure you want to stick around for the summer?" Having a retired nurse would help Evelyn's anxiety.

"I took care of my Richard at the end. Being there for someone who is about to take their last living breath is a privilege and an honor." Bitty's cheeks puffed out as she blew out a long breath. "Don't get me wrong, it's mighty hard. But to help take some of the fear away . . ."

"I offered her to stay with me for my own selfish reasons." Tears sprang to Evelyn's eyes. "When she said she was all alone . . . I am too. This loneliness permeates around me, weighing on me and pulling me down, and I feel like I'm drowning some days."

"It really is fate, because I've been feeling mighty lonely since I've lost Richard," Bitty said. "I thought meeting someone would make coming home to a dark, empty house better. Since I retired, there are too many days where I don't see another human being. And longer if I'm not counting the girl behind the grocery store register."

"My daughters call every once in a while, but not regularly. And I get it, but I spent years doing whatever I could to make them happy. I miss the busy we had as a family." Evelyn had expected to grow old with George and her daughters and their families. "I'm happy for them. But I don't want to go back to an empty house anymore."

"I hear you," Bitty said. "I moved into Richard's family's house, and they say they don't mind me staying there, but I have no ties, no connections there anymore."

Evelyn let out a chuckle at the coincidence. Who would have thought that, by leaving, she would find someone who knew exactly how she felt? It had to be serendipity.

"Stay for the summer at least," she said. "And the fall is incredible here."

Bitty smiled wide. "Let's help our friend together."

CHAPTER 12

*H*arper sat at her father's kitchen stool and drank his coffee. She put the mug on the table and dropped her book. "Why did you run off like that last night?"

After all that talk about being cool with Harper, Charlie had been the one who lost it.

"I felt like an idiot being there, and I reacted." He dropped his head back looking up to the ceiling, wishing he could do so many things over with that woman.

"Do you regret things?" Harper asked, slanting her eyes.

Charlie shook his head. "I don't regret how things turned out, but I regret how I behaved when things went wrong."

"What happened?" Harper asked.

"Come on, Harper, this is weird." He pushed back his chair from the kitchen table.

"Why?"

"Because you're my daughter, and talking about your mother and my relationships is weird."

"I'm just going to bother you until you do tell, so you might as well."

He heaved out a sigh. "Fine. After we got engaged, I got the job in Hollywood. Evelyn had just been accepted into the master's program at Emerson in Boston. It was her dream, and I had my dream, and we tried to make it work . . ."

"Then you met mom?" she asked. He could see her head working, piecing together the puzzle of her life story.

"It's a lot more complicated."

"But is it?" she asked.

She was right. It wasn't really complicated. He and Evelyn grew apart, they spent more time away from each other than they did together. They both didn't know what was going on with their lives and didn't have the money to live across the country from each other and make it work. There were a million other reasons why it didn't work out.

"I was stupid and jealous and not mature enough to make something like a long-distance relationship work."

He shook his head. He didn't need to tell her about it. It would only make things awkward between her and Evelyn.

CHAPTER 13

*E*velyn and Bitty found a furniture shop on Boylston Street right down from Copley Square in the heart of Boston. It had exactly what Evelyn needed.

"We can help with furnishing and design," the woman behind the desk said.

"I want to stay away from any ocean motif. Just soft earth tones and modern lines." Evelyn walked around the showroom and pointed to things she liked and walked past things she didn't. Never in her life had she felt comfortable spending money. Even though her parents had done well for themselves, they taught her how to pinch pennies and save. She saved for her own reasonable car. She saved for her apartment and spending during college. She saved when she and George moved back home with her parents when he first started practicing.

When she started earning more money with her books, and then even more when the television series came out, and even more after it became a major hit, they never really changed their lifestyle. She was still frugal. They stayed in their moderate house in the suburbs. They splurged with their cabin, but they sold it when the girls moved away. They always talked about traveling and getting a summer home on the water somewhere, but they never actually followed through.

What good did scrimping and scraping do once you were dead?

She would spend her money on living.

"I need some convalescent care furniture," she said. "A bed that's easy to get in and out, sit up. Also, toiletry items, a shower seat."

"I can help you find what you need." The saleswoman got right to business. Whoever said the younger generations were lazy didn't see this young lady get to work after Evelyn explained their circumstances.

"I can get the furniture started at the warehouse this afternoon, but it'll take a day or two to get it up to New England from where it's built in North Carolina."

Evelyn's stomach fluttered with butterflies. When they left the furniture store, she texted Harper, who called right away.

"He's available whenever you need," she said, referring to her construction contact.

Evelyn was going against her best judgment. She had no references. She hadn't seen any of his work. She was literally taking the word of a twenty-eight-year-old stranger. The contractor she recommended had been free to work anytime, which meant he didn't have much work. Was it like Harper said, that he had gone off on his own and didn't have a strong clientele or the reputation yet? Or was it that this guy didn't know what he was doing?

"He said he can meet me tomorrow?" Evelyn asked Harper while she and Bitty headed back to the hospital.

"I sent you all his information in the text."

"That's perfect." She had quite a bit of work she'd like done and wanted whoever Harper was recommending knowing what they were in for.

Harper didn't seem to be worried about it. "You'll love Mateo."

"Great, then please pass my information along." She hung up the phone and took in a deep breath before letting it out. An energy pulsed through her veins, and she wanted to do more. She turned to Bitty. "Did you want to try to attend the dinner tonight?"

"Nope." Bitty stopped walking and took hold of Evelyn's arm. "Girl, you need to slow down."

Evelyn's forehead creased. "Am I walking too fast?"

She hadn't thought she had been.

"No. All of this." Bitty flung her arms out with the furniture catalogs. "This is a lot to do. Are you sure you're able to take all this on?"

"Are you willing to stay and help?" she asked. Bitty had joined in during the moment, but was she second-guessing her decision?

"I will stay for the summer, but my son usually needs some help with the kids when school starts, what with winter and the holidays."

"Of course." Evelyn understood. "I didn't make you do this, did I?"

"Oh, heavens no." Bitty shook her head. "I'm always looking for an adventure. My son thinks I'm crazy."

"You already discussed this with him?" Evelyn had purchased a home, and everyone else knew except for her daughters. What did that say about their relationship?

Bitty rubbed Evelyn's arm. "Listen, since I'm in the passenger's seat of this journey of yours, I get a different perspective, and I see you pressing the gas, but not much of the brakes. Don't forget to slow down on those curves."

"Isn't that the time to speed up?" she teased. She patted Bitty's hand. "The more I go with my gut—deciding to come to Martha's Vineyard, buying the beach house, having you and Wanda stay—the more alive I've felt in years."

"Me too, to be honest." Bitty stared off but with a smile on her face. "Since I lost Richard, it's just been routine. I wake up and have breakfast. Watch the news. Have lunch. Run an errand. Have dinner. Watch the news. Go to bed. Wake up and have breakfast, watch the news . . ."

"God, it's the same with me." Evelyn looked out the store front. "Let's take a break and sit at the park."

She brought Bitty down toward Copley Square. The sounds of the city bounced off the stone and glass buildings. Cars jammed the streets, and people rushed down the sidewalks. Evelyn remembered how much she loved living in Boston.

"I miss the familiar adventures." She thought about when she had first started dating George. "George did his residence at Tufts." She pointed in the crow's direction to Tufts Hospital. "It's right in Chinatown. I'd ride the T to meet him for lunch during his shift, and we'd go to a new restaurant every time, comparing it to the previous one. We did that throughout our whole relationship—go to a restaurant, then score it to the others. I miss that more than anything. That ritual. That thing that made us, us."

She had met George at the hospital. Her roommate had fallen down their apartment staircase and broke her ankle. He had been the resident on staff in the emergency room. By the time her roommate was bandaged up, she had a date.

That night, Charlie had called her. They had been broken up for months, and she hadn't picked up. She'd let it go to her answering machine. Maybe she should've answered it. Maybe if she had, thirty years later, she'd have closure to that part of her life.

She never spoke to Charlie again.

She had almost completely forgotten about him.

Almost.

Evelyn and Bitty sat with Wanda in her hospital room. She slept most of the time, but the color in her face had returned with fluids, and the doctor said she'd be discharged within a few days.

"We'll have a room all set up," Evelyn explained. "I have a contractor coming out."

Wanda looked from Evelyn to Bitty. "I have nothing to offer."

"Oh, hubble squash," Bitty said.

"We're the sisterhood of misfits," Evelyn said. "Fate has anchored us together on that island. Now, let's ride this out together."

Wanda reached out to both ladies and squeezed their hands. When the nurse came in to check her vitals, the pair snuck out. Evelyn and Bitty got in their car and drove toward the ferry. They could make the last trip back to the island if there wasn't any traffic during rush hour.

"What should I expect?" she asked Bitty as the reality of taking care of Wanda hit her.

"She's going to be tired." Bitty let out a long breath, tapping the wheel with her thumbs. "And that woman is already a small, little thing, which tells me she's already having trouble eating."

Evelyn thought of all the times Wanda had been tired. How she didn't eat much, if at all, when they had been together. All the times when Wanda needed to rest or use the restroom.

"Do you think she skipped her treatment to come on this trip?" Evelyn wondered why Wanda would leave her medical team in Palm Springs if she knew she was that sick.

"I think this is exactly where she's supposed to be," Bitty said. "Now she has a world-renowned hospital taking care of her."

"And us," Evelyn said.

Bitty leaned back in the seat. "Yes, she has us."

They made the second to last ferry in plenty of time. Bitty suggested a tea, and they climbed up to the top floor of the ferry and Bitty elbowed her lightly in the arm.

"Looks like fate is playing some more games." She pointed to a man standing at the coffee counter.

Charlie froze when he saw her staring at him.

She walked toward him. He still hadn't moved.

"Charlie," she said when she got close.

"Evelyn. I didn't see you get on." He said it as though he shouldn't be there.

"I didn't see you either," she said. She pointed behind her to Bitty. "Do you remember my friend?"

"Yes. Bitty, right?" he asked. Behind him, the sun hung low over the water. The city of Falmouth started to glow in the distance.

"Yes, that's right," she said in her southern drawl.

"I was just getting coffee."

"This late?" Bitty tsked with her tongue. "I'd be up all night. Speaking of which, I should hit the restroom real quick."

Bitty took off through the crowd toward the bathrooms, leaving Charlie and Evelyn standing alone.

"I took Harper's advice, and I'm meeting the contractor tomorrow at the house," she said, hoping that would ease the tension.

"Mateo?" He laughed, and her concern at his humor must've shown on her face, because he stopped and held out his hands. "He's great. I'm laughing because I think she has a little crush on him. So, to hear she recommended him . . ."

He looked at her, the light reflecting in his deep honey eyes. The local boy she had a crush on, who had this aura, this rugged, Beat Generation thing about him. He could throw a punch and drink beer but talk literature. He drove a motorcycle when she first met him but also took care of his aunt's flower garden and wrote poetry. He worked in the back of the restaurant but could mingle with the guests. Now in his fifties, he was still just as attractive, if not more so, and he still had that elusive manner about him.

He also wrote her favorite book of all time.

And she was certain it was about her.

"Harper told me to come to the next writers' group."

"You want to come back to our little writers' group?" His surprise bothered her because it meant he no longer knew her. Of course she'd want to be part of an intimate group of creatives. That's the kind of thing she enjoyed, but her agent and her publicist and her publishing house wanted her to go to large conferences, put her name in for big awards she had no business chasing. Let the new writers get recognition. Give awards to those who were changing things, not keeping it the same.

"You'll have to bring a piece of writing."

She jerked her head back, and let out a laugh. "Seriously?"

"Nobody's special, not even fancy published authors." He smiled at her. "I'm kidding. You don't have to bring anything if you don't want to."

"Of course I'll bring something." She remembered his rules of engagement from years ago. She had to prove herself. And it was about time she proved herself *for* herself.

"I'm sorry if I upset you the other day." He played with his coffee's top.

She held the strap of her purse, rubbing her thumb against its leather. "I'm sorry too. I have a lot of emotions these days."

"Really?" He winked. "I hadn't noticed."

"But I'm learning to lean into those around me." She thought about Bitty and Wanda and Harper. "And since we're going to be neighbors . . ."

When Bitty came walking back, he smiled and jerked up his cup of coffee. "Well, enjoy the ride back to the island. I think I'll grab a seat."

Bitty called out as he walked away. "You should join us."

But he shook his head. He gave another wave and took off.

She watched as he went toward the stairs. The summer night was still light and warm as the sun began its descent. Just as she was about to let him take off, a seagull flew beside the ferry window, gliding on the wind. It swooped through the air, swaying from side to side, gliding along with the ferry.

"Dang it, George," she said out loud, and even though Bitty heard, she didn't ask. Evelyn turned to where Charlie took off. "Charlie! Wait up!"

He stopped as soon as she said his name.

"Join us on the deck," she said to him as he faced her. "We're going to catch the sunset."

He smiled. "That sounds nice."

They sat on the deck under the canopy, and they explained their adventure of the last few days.

"So, you all just randomly took this trip for singles?" He seemed interested in the idea that they went along with a singles' retreat to Martha's Vineyard but had no desire to meet anyone.

"It was a free trip." Bitty flew up her arms as if she didn't really understand herself. "I haven't had real good seafood in years."

Bitty sure was fun, and Evelyn felt proud to have a friend like her, sitting there with Charlie. She had forgotten how witty he was and laughed as he and Bitty continued with their friendly banter.

"What exactly do you do at these singles' events?" he asked.

Bitty slapped her knee and said, "Why don't you come and find out."

CHAPTER 14

*W*ith all the time that had passed, Charlie wondered if Evelyn had changed, and as he sat there at a table in a large reception room for the singles' night event, smelling her scent of rose and vanilla and something sweet he couldn't name, he realized she had, very much so. She had evolved like a caterpillar into a butterfly. Her beauty had always been there, but she had become a strong and fierce force.

"You're amazing," he said to her after she finished telling him of her plan with the beach house and how they were going to help Wanda get through treatment together.

Her face flushed, and she shifted in her seat. "I wouldn't call me amazing."

"She is, isn't she?" Bitty said. "I suppose she was like this as a girl."

He shook his head. "The same, but different."

"How so?" Evelyn smiled, her eyes twinkling.

"She was shy and lacked confidence," he began. "But when I first met her, she came off as aloof."

"You mean a snob?" Bitty corrected him.

"Talk about calling the kettle black," Evelyn came back at him. She turned to Bitty. "He drove this little motorcycle around the island saying things like *The salt's in my blood* and *I'm too cool for school.*"

He laughed. "I was such a jerk back then."

"You hated me from the minute I walked into the restaurant at The Wharf."

Charlie raised his finger in the air. "As I recall, someone said they hailed from Dartmouth."

Bitty's head followed the argument from Charlie to Evelyn. "Where's Dartmouth?"

"Hanover," they answered at the same time.

"What's wrong with saying the college name where I lived and went to school?" she asked as if he were being unreasonable.

"Because people using their Ivy League college's name as a location is just pointing out that they attend an Ivy League college."

"Is it wrong to be proud of what you accomplished?" she asked.

Their voices were light and teasing, but he wondered if he was pushing her buttons and it was irritating her, or did it excite her like it did him, having this back and forth? He decided not to push it and return to a normal conversation for at least her friend's sake.

"Let's test those Ivy League skills out at the writers' group," he said. "It's small, but everyone takes the meetings seriously."

"What if I come as Evelyn Flannery?" she asked.

"That would be great." He didn't know how one person could affect him like she did, but something about the way she looked at him, catching him, making him keep her stare, was intoxicating. She demanded his attention, yet did nothing more than give him a look. Maybe it was animalistic, as if her pheromones captured him, and his instincts took over.

But rational thought said to stay friendly, neighborly. Yes, she bought a beach house, but that wasn't a declaration of love. She bought a house in the most beautiful place on earth, where he happened to live.

She had changed. Maybe she just liked Harper and wanted to be friendly for his daughter's sake. Maybe she felt sorry for him. Or maybe she did still have some feelings for him.

He was determined to find out.

When the dance floor started slowing down, Bitty said good night to them both.

"You're leaving?" Evelyn said, as though she were afraid of being left alone with Charlie.

"I'm beat," Bitty said. "I need to call my son, find a pet sitter, and get some rest, and all in that order."

"Walk tomorrow morning?" Evelyn asked.

"Sounds good." Bitty waved to Charlie. "Nice seeing you again."

"Come to the writers' group as well," he offered.

"Oh dear, that's not a good idea for anyone." She clapped her hand on her chest. "I'm afraid I'm not very creative in that area."

"Everyone has a story to tell, and writing is just another way to communicate it."

"Thanks for the invitation, I'll think about it." Bitty smiled, grabbed her purse, and headed out of the restaurant.

"This place has really changed," Charlie said, looking around the old stomping grounds.

He could almost imagine the old days of them running around the restaurant, working all day and staying up all night to just do it again. "How did we even have time to hang out back then?"

"I don't know," she said.

Silence suddenly hung around them like fog on the ocean's surface.

"I'm glad you invited me. Thank you." He wanted her to know he was sincere. "And thank you about Harper."

"You've thanked me enough," she said back, and he wasn't sure how to take it. Her tone was indifferent.

He bit his bottom lip, planning out what he wanted to say before he put his foot in his mouth.

"Why did you come back?" He blurted out and by the look on Evelyn's face, he should've kept his mouth shut, because she wasn't ready to discuss it. "I mean, did you really come for a singles' vacation to write?"

Maybe she did. Maybe he was too hopeful she came to find some peace in their past. He waited for her to respond, but when she didn't, he rose out of his chair. He didn't need to push things between them. "It's been a nice night."

"I needed a change." She didn't elaborate, which he took as she didn't want to discuss it with him.

"Well, thanks anyway for helping Harper like you have." As he stood, she put her hand on his arm.

"Please." The touch from Evelyn's hand had been hot, radiating up his body. "Stay."

He slowly lowered into the seat.

"Harper says you hardly write anymore."

He assumed she was asking it like a question, but it was a statement. A fact. A testament. He hadn't written in years.

"I just lost it." There was nothing more to say. He didn't have the story within him at this point, and he hated a sequel or a cookie-cutter plot that the industry loved.

"You were always that writer who needed to *feel* it." She raised her eyebrow. "Do you still just write to discover?"

"Of course." He never understood how someone could plan and plan and spend all that time to have to write it out essentially twice. "Why go through the journey a second time?"

"Because sometimes the story needs a second chance," she said.

A pause in the conversation made him wonder if she was no longer talking about writing.

Then she asked, "Why don't you write?"

He guessed she hadn't let her feelings go. Her coldness, then warmth was confusing. First, she wants nothing to do with him, then coffee, then she walks out, then she invites him into her new house? "Why won't you forgive me?"

She sat up, her back straight, her lips pursed in a tight line, and she played with the stem of her drink.

"I've forgiven you," she said, "and I hope you've forgiven me as well."

Forgiven her? He thought her disdain toward him was her holding a grudge all this time. She wanted him to forgive her?

"You have nothing to be forgiven for." He shook his hands out. "Nothing whatsoever."

"The truth is, I came here to change my life." Her shoulders fell and she sat back. "My girls have lives of their own. I'm rotting away in a life that died five years ago. I am—" She stopped suddenly. She let out a long sigh. "I'm finally ready to go and discover who I am now."

He couldn't hold back his smile. "Change is like a roller coaster, and you always hated roller coasters."

"I'm not looking for thrills. I just want a change." She gazed out the dark window. "I want to wake up looking forward to something."

He waited to see if she had more to say.

"I haven't written a story, a complete story, in five years." She blew out. "And I haven't told a soul."

"So you're writing, but just not finishing anything?" That was unlike her from what he remembered, but a very common situation. Did she suffer from the shiny new object syndrome and start new stories when a new idea came to mind? Or was it the overedit syndrome when nothing was ever perfect enough to move on?

"I can't write happy endings anymore."

"Ah." His heart plunged and understood the crux. Romance always has a happy ending.

"Then don't." He shrugged.

"Evelyn Rose is about hope and the happily ever afters." She looked back at him. "I don't have it in me to create those fantasies."

Evelyn had always been the quiet thunder that shook the

world below. She blew her career out of the water. She was the definition of success. She could literally walk away, never write again, and be declared a hero in this business. Someone who set out and accomplished exactly what she had set out to do. And here he was, stuck in the same spot as he had been years ago.

"You're killing it. Why not spin directions, and do something that fits you now as a writer?"

He knew George was her happily ever after. He was the one who came in on the white horse, who saved her from the jerk who left for his dream. He had been the antagonist in her stories. The guy who broke the heroine's heart. The guy who trampled on her self-worth, her confidence, and her ability to trust. He was the guy who ruined love for her main character, and George was the hero who saved her.

And she'd lost him. Forever.

Or maybe . . . ? Could he be the hero she needs now?

"Let's get out of here," he said, "and go to the beach. Take a walk."

She shook her head. "I have a big day tomorrow. I should get some rest."

As she was about to stand, he took her hand in between both of his. "Come and work on your writing with the group."

She looked at him, but something caught her eye. Her hand went to his shoulder, and she pulled off a tiny feather stuck to his sports coat. She laughed and placed it in her palm, then blew on it. She smiled, taking back his hand, her eyes holding his. He didn't let go, even though neighbors didn't hold hands that long, and friends didn't send electricity through his body.

"I should go." She dropped his hand and picked up her purse.

Before he could call out, she was gone.

CHAPTER 15

*W*hen Evelyn finally agreed to go on the trip to Martha's Vineyard, she had been at her lowest. She remembered waking up with nothing to write, staring at her screen in the same clothes she wore to bed—and wore the day before. She hadn't showered and couldn't remember when she last did. She looked at her phone and realized she hadn't returned her sister's messages for three days. Just when she thought of an excuse to text Carol as to why she couldn't go on a singles' trip to Martha's Vineyard, a cardinal flew into her living room window. The loud pound against the glass made her drop her phone on her computer. She got up and hurried to the door and ran outside. The bird lay still on the ground.

"Oh no," she said, kneeling on the ground next to it. "Please don't be dead."

Was it safe to touch? Didn't birds have diseases? Should she call a bird rescue person or a veterinarian?

"Okay, little birdie, let's see if you're alright."

With a jerk, the bird came to and shook its wings, fanning them out and stretching its feathers. But the bird must've been in shock because it didn't move.

The cardinal sat there, its shiny black eyes reflecting her

image back at her. She saw herself, and suddenly a sob escaped her. She didn't recognize the sound that came out of her body, but she broke down because she didn't like the person looking back. When had she lost hope? When had she given up? Why didn't she love herself anymore?

A moan broke out of her chest, and she couldn't believe it came from her. It sounded as though someone had ripped out her heart. More groans escaped as she wrapped her arms around her waist and rocked back and forth, trying to hold herself together; otherwise, she was sure she'd fall apart.

All the while, the bird didn't move.

It stayed still, not letting go of her stare. Its vulnerability in lying there made her lose her emotions.

"You have to fly away." She hiccupped as she tried to catch her breath, but the pain was like a vise around her lungs. "You can't stay here."

The bird's head tilted at her sound, but it didn't stir.

"What do I do?" she asked through sobs. "Do you need help?"

Then, as if nothing had happened, the bird flew off.

She watched as it flew to a nearby pine and landed on a branch. The tree was a set of hemlocks George had planted the first summer they lived in the house.

"What should I do to help me?" The words came out hard.

She stayed on her knees; she didn't think she could stand, the emptiness crippling. She had everything in her life, and it vanished.

"I hate being alone," she said to the bird. "I hate it."

Tears stung her eyes, blurring the bird's reds into the evergreen of the pine. "I am so alone."

The house was too big for one person, her daughters weren't coming back, George's ashes had been spread—nothing was holding her there.

The cardinal flew off, and she got up to follow it as it flew to another hemlock. "Please help me," she begged. "Please tell me what I should do."

The bird flew across the lawn to the neighbor's yard. That's when she swore the darn thing looked back at her.

"Fly away?"

She fell back to the ground and palmed the grass in her hands. She needed to fly away. Make a serious change in her life. The second the cardinal flew out of sight, she got up and walked straight into the house and called her sister.

"Carol," she said over the phone, her voice panicked.

"Evie?" Her sister sounded like she was at a restaurant. "Everything okay?"

"I'll go on the trip."

"You will?" Carol sounded excited.

"Do you really think it'll be good for me?" she asked.

Their last conversation had been heated. Carol was the one who had pointed out her sweatpants she continued to wear, her lack of interest in all things, and how she wasn't leaving the house.

She had hit rock bottom.

But in the moment after she hung up, she knew she had to change things if she was going to survive.

With the windows open in her hotel room, and the sound of the waves flowing through them, Evelyn stared at that stupid cursor on her computer, at three a.m. once again, she decided to just go for it.

And she wrote.

The last thing I said to my husband was, "Pick up your underwear."

And Evelyn began to type. One word here, another two there. Soon she had a paragraph. Then a few pages of her own love story.

By six a.m., she met Bitty outside her room in her walking shoes, and they took off, walking down the beach toward the beach house.

"Sure is a pretty sunrise today," Bitty said. "I'm looking forward to waking up to this every morning."

Evelyn could feel a pitter-patter in her heart. "I'm real grateful you agreed to stay."

"I think we're all a bit crazy, but hey, if Dorothy, Blanche, and Rose can do it . . ."

"Don't forget about Sophia." She pointed her finger at Bitty.

Bitty let out a chuckle. "I wonder who that'd end up being."

Evelyn could see the beach house coming into view. "I can't believe I bought it."

"I've never owned my own home—always a renter. As a traveling nurse, I never had the time to take care of a house."

"That must've been hard moving around so much." Evelyn had always been a homebody. She liked roots. She liked familiarity. It wasn't a surprise that her change and journey would be in a familiar place she had already lived.

"I loved it." Bitty looked ahead. "I loved meeting new people, going different places. I only settled down because I fell in love."

"I'm sorry you lost Richard."

"Oh, girl. Don't I know it." She shook her head. "I'm sure sorry you lost your George."

Bitty hooked her arm in Evelyn's; their eight-inch difference didn't seem to make them off balance which tickled Evelyn. She patted her arm.

They walked as they went over the plans for the day. At eight, Evelyn would be meeting the contractor Harper had recommended. After, they were going to hit the local shops for some fun touches. She wanted to spend some time planning out Wanda's space so she would be comfortable, but also Bitty's as well. She didn't want them feeling like guests but as honored members of her family. She wanted them to feel at home.

Her heroine needed sidekicks.

Women who understood what she was going through. She loved her sister, but Carol lived in Colorado with her younger children and happy husband. The girls certainly didn't want to live in a sleepy midwestern town or an isolating island where there was hardly any nightlife and was completely empty in the winter.

"You know, I really liked Charlie," Bitty said as they reached the wooden staircase that led to the beach house's planked walkway.

Evelyn couldn't help but smile. "He's a charmer."

"There's something about him. He's mysterious—those intriguing eyes." Bitty went ahead of her up the stairs. "He's easy to talk to as well."

"He's an incredible writer." After all the money Evelyn spent on college and getting her MFA, she learned everything from him during those summers. How to pace, how to lead the reader through the character's mind, how to draw out suspense and tease the climax to the perfect peak.

"Says the incredible writer," Bitty said. "Though the last few books . . . they were different."

Evelyn hadn't really thought about Bitty being a reader, but only someone who was a superfan would see the difference in writing.

"How'd you know?" How many other fans was she losing through this?

"It felt different." Bitty shrugged, walking along, her footsteps a deep echo from the wood. "Just off."

"I wrote them when I was young, before George." Heartbroken Evelyn had written those manuscripts, which widowed and inconsolable Evelyn Rose had edited and sent to her editor. They were so hungry to get something out that they'd ignored the glaring differences. Her writing had been flowery and over-written. She'd told what was happening instead of showing it through the story. She'd made rookie errors—used too many adjectives and overused the infamous adverbs.

"I think Charlie may still have feelings for you." Bitty winked. "How do you feel about that?"

She didn't know how to feel. "I think he's in love with

someone else. Someone who left this island and never came back." Evelyn pulled out her key and unlocked the door. She stepped inside the house, and a musky, tangy sea scent filled her nose. She could feel her chest expand in excitement just as anxiety ran up her legs. She wasn't the girl she had been back then, and if Charlie expected that Evelyn, he would be sadly disappointed.

"I say you give it a try," Bitty said, walking to the bathroom.

Evelyn pulled out a roll of toilet paper from her backpack and handed it to her.

"What you got to lose?" Bitty said as she closed the door.

"That's exactly what frightens me," Evelyn whispered to herself. The very thought of losing another person had kept her up at night since she'd arrived on the island. "He taught me that even nice guys can hurt the ones they love."

"Shoot. That's heavy," Bitty said as she came out of the bathroom.

Bitty headed back to the hotel as Evelyn stayed and waited for the contractor. Mateo greeted her with a hearty handshake.

"Thank you so much for meeting me on such short notice," she said.

"It all happened to be perfect timing," he said. "I just had a house reno fall through when its permits were denied."

She smiled. He did have work. "Do you have a portfolio of work?"

He handed her a card. "You can check out my website and see all my projects there. My sister-in-law runs the office, and she'd be happy to show you our past projects."

This news was music to her ears. She was working with a professional contractor. "Well, Mateo, I've got big plans for this old place."

She walked Mateo through the house. She had hoped the structure wasn't as bad as she thought, but based on Mateo's expression, she was wrong. It was worse.

"Have you had this place inspected?" he asked.

She shook her head.

"And you bought it on the spot?" He glanced around the small kitchen.

"Yes." She waited for him to say something. Her heart pounded in her chest.

"I think you made the right decision," he said, taking a photo with his phone and typing something.

"Really?" she let out a nervous laugh.

"You don't see old places like this anymore. They were built to last, and they've been tearing them down to build these monstrosities. I think you'll be happy with your decision."

Her stomach left her throat as relief settled over her.

"That's so good to hear." She let out another chuckle. "I thought I had bought myself a money pit."

"You have a lot of work ahead of you, but from what I can see, it's cosmetic—a lot of interior work. The electrical needs to be updated, the plumbing. The flooring may have to be looked at." He jumped on the linoleum. "But the structure is solid, built strong to withstand whatever comes through the island."

She placed her hands on her waist. "Where would you start first? Keeping in mind I have my friends staying here as well, and we'll all be in need of a bathroom and kitchen right away."

"I can start in the bathroom." They walked to the full bath located in the front.

"My hope is to extend the living room and open it up to the porch." She walked into the guest bedroom that had two small windows and pine paneling throughout. "I'd also like to make the downstairs bathroom handicap accessible."

He took notes on his phone as she spoke, asking questions here and there, explaining what he would have to do.

"What's the budget?" he asked.

Evelyn stood there and realized that this was the first time she had done something like this ever in her life. She had never bought a house and certainly hadn't hired a contractor to work on a house she really had no business buying. She had expected

Mateo to think she was crazy or at least naïve, but he seemed to respect her decisions and even agree with her plans. All her life, she had someone to do everything for her. Her agent negotiated her contracts, her book deals, her movie rights. George did everything else from paying the bills to buying her cars. Donna, her assistant, took care of everything else. Evelyn glided through life, never making any adult decision on her own.

It was about time.

"I also want to extend the back." She knew this would be harder than she expected. "I assume I'd have to go to the city about that?"

He nodded. "Being in the hills and along the shore like you are, they are really relentless with the codes and building permits. But it's not impossible."

She would like to add another full bathroom on the second floor so each of the final three bedrooms would have a full bath. Her goal was to make the house as inviting and welcoming as possible for her guests to feel comfortable. She wanted them to want to stay.

"How long will it take to get the bathrooms and kitchen in shape?" Evelyn hoped it wouldn't take too long.

"I'd say a couple of months."

"Could you find a few extra hands if I paid for it?" she asked.

He nodded. "I could find a few more guys."

"I'd really like to get the bathrooms done first," she said.

"Sure, I'll get right on it." He shook her hand. "I can start by ordering supplies this afternoon."

She picked up her phone and texted Harper after Mateo left.

Thanks for the recommendation! Mateo is perfect.

Dots flashed across the screen on Harper's end. A heart emoji popped up on the screen and then, **He's the best. I think you'll be very happy with him. See you tonight!**

See you tonight? Evelyn thought. Then she remembered. The writers' club was tonight.

She stood alone in the beach house, and the urge to write

made her take out her phone, and she began to dictate. She had tried so many times in the past to dictate, but it never worked well for her. Her thoughts worked better with her fingers, not her speech. But there she was, pacing the floors of her new living room, getting her ideas out with ease, like the wind along the water's surface. She couldn't hear the waves off in the distance, but she could feel the wind and the cries of seagulls swooping overhead. She opened all the windows and dictated her story for the rest of the morning, even trying to do it in the car on the way back to The Wharf.

She skipped the luncheon, which Bitty said was decent.

"I got stuck sitting next to Mitch," she said and laughed at the coincidence.

"Tomorrow, we're headed out at seven for Wanda," she reminded Bitty.

"Sounds good to me," Bitty said.

The rest of the afternoon, she revised her first chapter over and over, polishing it to the point of overpolishing and deleting four hundred words. What was with her? Was she ready to show herself like this? Expose her darkest parts of her soul? Who wanted to read about a woman falling apart? Would anyone be sympathetic, even? She didn't have a bad life. She was lucky. She made a comfortable living, and was able to buy a house by the sea. She had two beautiful daughters and a very successful career, even if she stopped at this point. She had a wonderful sister and a family who she adored. She had nothing to complain about.

"You came," Charlie said. He smiled as she walked into Martha's Mysteries and toward the small group of men and women sitting in a circle. Some held glasses of wine, while others drank coffee. The group was an eclectic mix of young and old. All had notebooks, computers, or books in their laps.

"Evelyn!" Harper waved from her seat and jumped up to greet her. "I heard from your agent."

"That's wonderful," she said as Harper reached in for a hug.

Evelyn giggled, literally feeling Harper's excitement shake her little body.

"She said she loved the first three chapters and wants to read the rest of the manuscript," Harper said.

Evelyn knew Sue would. This was the passing of the guard. Evelyn was handing Sue her new writer. "Would you like me to help with editing?"

Harper squeezed her again. "Are you kidding? Yes, I would love that."

The group either didn't seem to notice the interaction or they were used to Harper's enthusiasm. She bet it was the latter.

As everyone found a seat, Charlie pulled an empty chair next to him and offered her the seat. Then he stood as others quieted down around them. "Welcome back, everyone," Charlie said, looking around at each of them. "Tonight, we have a special guest. I'd like you all to meet an old friend—"

"Who are you calling old?" Evelyn teased.

He smiled. "My beautiful friend, Evelyn."

"Welcome, Evelyn," they said.

"Would you like some wine?" A woman, who looked in her forties, held up a bottle of red.

"You know, I would love a glass," she said. She could feel her nerves as she sat there.

"You know about the first rule?" the woman asked as she poured the drink.

"Yes, Charlie told me," Evelyn said.

Newbies had to read first.

"We haven't had someone new come in years." She handed her a plastic cup with the wine.

"Thanks," Evelyn said as she took a sip, her heart pounding in her chest. When was the last time she allowed herself to be this vulnerable?

"Are we ready to begin?" Charlie asked.

A man who looked like he was in his later years passed a plate of cookies over to her. "My wife made them this morning. I'm Hank."

"Thank you," she said, picking up a chocolate chip.

"Charlie says you're moving to the island," Hank said.

She nodded. "Yes, I bought a house on Cliffside Point in the hills."

Hank whistled. "Gorgeous spot. The old Buckley place, right?"

"Yes." Martha's Vineyard was a big island, but one small town. She hadn't forgotten how small of a town it was.

She had been grateful Charlie kept her information private, allowing her new neighbors to find out who she was before learning *who* she was.

"Are you a snowbird, then?" he asked.

"More like a seagull just trying to find a good spot to land." She rolled her eyes inside her head at her ridiculous simile amongst a group of figurative language junkies.

"Welcome, John Livingston Seagull," Hank teased, and a laugh erupted from her belly.

"I like you, Hank." She took a sip of her wine and realized the whole group stared at her, waiting for her to begin. "Oh, sorry. Do I need to explain or anything?"

An elderly woman, who had to be at least in her late eighties, early nineties, shook her head. "Just read."

She set her drink down and lifted her chapter in her hands. She hadn't read in front of a group of people in years. Yet, she wasn't nervous—not like when she didn't know what she was doing, but more anxious about how strangers would receive it. She had been padded for years from a wonderful, hard-working, devoted team. She and her agent had been together longer than the length of her marriage. She didn't know if what she wrote had worked so much that it wasn't even her writing in the end. Did she still have it? Has she grown as a novelist? Or was she behaving like a Real Housewife with a glam squad behind her, making her look the part, but not able to do it on her own?

Her stomach swirled as she licked her lips and began.

CHAPTER 16

*C*harlie sat in awe as Evelyn read her chapter. From the looks on everyone's faces, they felt the same way. She didn't just read. No, Evelyn performed her work like a stage actress. She had people laughing right away but broke their hearts within the same first sentence.

He realized it was a sort-of fictionalized memoir with the names of the characters changed. After she finished, like always, the group started with feedback with the person to her left.

Which was Charlie.

He usually took this role so that others could hear his way of critiquing. People liked to be nice, not constructive. He of all people knew writers needed to push their feelings aside and hear the good, the bad, and the ugly.

But tonight, he held back before speaking. He glanced around the group; some of them were drying their eyes. Harper blew her nose. Evelyn, not breaking a sweat, hadn't broken from the character who narrated the story the whole reading.

"It's beautiful," he said right away. He was the one who hadn't written a word in years. Should he really be the one handing over criticism? She obviously had a masterpiece by the reaction from the others. But he had to be honest. "But it doesn't sound like you."

She sat back, putting the chapter in her lap. "It doesn't sound like me?"

Harper shot him a look. "It's a story, isn't it?"

"I thought it was wonderful," Anita said from the other side of the circle.

"Yes, but . . ." They thought Evelyn had just walked off the street, not that she was Evelyn Rose, New York Times Best Seller. "If you're here for a critique, that's my critique. You held back."

She stared back at him as the group stayed quiet. "I held back?" She looked curious. "Where?"

He flipped through the first two pages and then read a few lines out loud. "Your character is distant, going through the motions. Which is a real thing when trauma happens, but you're hitting the perfect emotions at the perfect time. It's romanticizing the terror."

He felt his face grimace as he spoke, but Evelyn's expression didn't change.

"I totally disagree," Harper shot out. "I think you hit the right emotions for the moment of discovery. She isn't going to laugh when a police officer tells her that her husband's just died."

As Evelyn listened, he noticed her playing with her hands, rubbing and squeezing. He wondered if he was pushing her. She had written about losing her husband, and he tells her it's not real enough?

"Okay, I'm probably just picking," he said, not willing to argue in front of everyone or embarrass Evelyn by being too hard. "It's beautiful writing, no matter what I say."

"No." She shifted in her seat to face him. "I want to know, really. What else did you notice?"

"I think you're being a bit harsh on the lady," Hank said to Charlie.

Evelyn shook her head, and a smile broke on her lips. "Charlie's right. I did hold back." She flipped the pages back to page one. "Where else?"

Everyone's eyes were on Charlie.

He took a deep breath, then said, "What was the first thought that wasn't about George at that moment?"

"What do you mean?" Evelyn asked.

"Who's George?" Anita asked.

"When you found out your husband died, what was the first thought that wasn't about him?"

She stared at him, and he wished he had stopped like Hank had suggested.

"I just remember, when I found out my father died," Charlie said. He had been just twenty-one and hadn't heard from him in years. "I was mad because the money I wanted to buy a bus ticket to see you had to go to his funeral instead." He could see expressions twisting with the new information. "It's selfish, wrong, to think about your girlfriend when you found out the worst news of your life. But it shows the character's human. She's perfect right now."

Evelyn sat back and looked at the chapter in her hands. Her fingers squeezed the papers, and he was about to apologize, when she began to laugh. "You did it again, Charlie Moran. You did it again."

"Did what?" Hank asked.

She didn't answer, just looked at him, her eyes narrowing slightly with a hint of mischief, but she didn't explain. Instead, the rest of the group sang her praises. No one followed Charlie's rule of constructive feedback. A few asked questions to get a deeper picture, but they offered no real revisions, and he didn't push it because, really, it was a masterpiece like everyone was saying.

Harper read next, and the group returned to normal. Anita suggested using more description at the beginning of the epilogue. Patrick suggested cutting down on description. Harper nodded and thanked everyone.

"Tell us about this agent," Anita said to her.

"It's all quite exciting, really." Harper crossed her legs on her seat, a habit she'd had since she was a little girl. "It's because Evelyn sent her agent my manuscript."

He wanted to slap his forehead. Oh, Harper.

Every head turned to Evelyn.

Harper then even followed through and said, "Didn't you know it's Evelyn Rose?"

Hank let out a laugh. "You're kidding?"

Anita smiled but went straight back to her knitting. "I loved your Vineyard series."

He saw Evelyn sneak a peek at him, but he pretended not to notice. Over the next few minutes, she answered questions, but none of the group gaped too much at the famous writer.

The rest of the evening, the group read and gave feedback. People stuck around longer than usual, probably because of the new celebrity in their midst, but he could tell Evelyn enjoyed her time as well.

When she set down her second empty glass of wine, she gave him a look that said she was leaving.

"You headed out?" he asked, though she had picked up her purse.

"Yes, I have a big day tomorrow."

"You're bringing your friend home, right?"

She nodded, pleased he had remembered. "We're taking the ferry in the morning."

He looked at the clock, wishing he had more time. "I hope I didn't offend you by my critiques."

She placed her hand on his and shook her head. "I can't tell you how grateful I am you said what you did." Her eyes glistened. "I needed a kick in the rear."

She patted him and waved. "Thank you for tonight. I really enjoyed myself."

"Tomorrow, then."

"Tomorrow what?" she asked.

"Dinner, with me." He held her stare. "I have the perfect spot."

She smiled, then frowned. "Tomorrow might not work with Wanda coming home."

His heart sunk.

"But how about the day after?"

A smile broke across his face. "That sounds great."

The next morning, Charlie sat at the bench outside the ticket station and waited for her. As she and her friend, Bitty, approached the entrance, she smiled the second she saw him.

"I thought it was a perfect day for a trip to the city," he said as they came closer.

Her face glowed when she smiled, and he could feel her radiance shining from within. He couldn't explain it, but there was something there, something they both hadn't lost over those years.

He followed the women up the plank to the ferry and bought them both a coffee. He enjoyed spending time with them. Bitty had a great sense of humor, and her southern take on things was endearing. He also found out how she had worked in emergency rooms throughout the country and went straight into disasters when others were trying to get out.

"I worked at Shriners in Galveston and in Boston," she said. "Just as a traveling nurse, but you get to know a lot of children and their families. I always tried to bring a little bit of hope every day to work."

He really liked Evelyn's friend.

"I think that's why I kept writing romance," Evelyn said. "I'd get so many letters from readers who said how my books helped them through hard times. That my book let them escape for a bit."

"That's what you're both giving Wanda," he said, still blown away by the generosity of the two women before him. "Hope."

Bitty smiled. "Yes, I guess we are." Then she asked, "Are you coming with us to the hospital?"

He shook his head. "No, I just thought I'd go for a boat ride."

The ferry slowed as it came to the docks. People stood in line, ready to board, as it came into the harbor.

"Are you just staying in the city?" Evelyn asked.

He'd love to explore the city one day with her. Take her to a Red Sox game or stroll through the Fine Arts museum.

"I'm afraid I have some errands and I have to head back." He just didn't want another morning not seeing her.

When Bitty excused herself to the restroom, Evelyn turned to him and said, "I remembered the roast in the oven."

"You have a roast in the oven?"

"No, it's what I thought after hearing about George," she responded. He could tell it was hard to admit for her. "Is that terrible?"

"I thought about cheating on Tanya when she told me about her first affair," Charlie said. "It's when I knew I hated her and no longer loved her. Isn't that terrible?"

"Did you?" she asked.

He shook his head. "No. I tried to make it work, did therapy, the whole nine yards. When she realized I wasn't going anywhere, that's when she left."

"I rewrote the whole chapter," she said. "And I'd really like you to take another look at it."

"Of course." He liked it when she showed her vulnerability, when she allowed her realness to shine through.

She pulled her phone from her purse and opened her home screen. "I've sent you a link to my document."

He felt the text's vibration from his phone. "Great. I'll have something to read on the way back."

She let out a laugh so melodious it sounded like a song.

"Nothing like reading about someone's spouse's death to get through a boat ride," she said, her laughter ending suddenly.

"It takes courage to write like this," he said, catching her eyes and holding them with his. The exact reason why he didn't write himself.

"Hardly. Most likely desperate." She wiped her palms along

her pant legs. "But I don't think I can write anything else until I write about this."

Her eyes held his for a moment longer, sending an energy throughout his body. Then suddenly, she broke away, her arm extended out, waving to Bitty.

The ferry stopped and she stood, putting her purse on her shoulder. "We're going to head straight to the hospital."

"I hope everything goes smoothly for Wanda," he said.

"Thank you," she said.

"Dinner still?" He hoped she hadn't changed her mind.

"I'm looking forward to hearing what you think during it." She held up her finger at him. "I want constructive criticism."

He held up his phone. "Can't wait."

She backed away as Bitty met up with her. She called out a goodbye, and the two took off to the cars below deck.

He opened the document as soon as he sat back down. He read the first sentence and caught his breath. She had changed it all. The whole tone of the piece was different. It was real, raw, and powerful.

"Holy schnikes," he said aloud as he wiped away a tear that had fallen before he even realized his emotions had gotten the better of him. He laughed, looking around to see if any of the traveling tourists spotted the local yokel crying on the top deck.

She had not only revised the whole piece, but when he finished, he needed to read more.

He texted her right away. **Send me the rest.**

He saw she was texting, or at least on the thread. The dots flashed but then stopped.

Nothing.

He waited, and when a few minutes had passed, he reminded himself she was traveling to Boston. She didn't have time to text him back.

When twenty minutes had passed, he could see the island and put his phone away. He had a lot to do, and sitting by his phone, waiting for a woman to text him, was not how he was going to spend the day.

But even with the mantra *do not check your phone* repeating in his mind, Charlie continuously checked his phone.

"Someone likes someone," Harper teased behind her book.

"Aren't you supposed to be stocking shelves?" he said to his daughter, whose feet rested on a coffee table.

"You know . . ." She put the book down and got up, beginning a Harper lecture.

He should've just let her keep reading.

"You two are really good together," she said.

Didn't he know it. "Your point?"

He wouldn't tell Harper about Evelyn sharing her writing with him. No, he'd keep a boundary with Harper about the things between him and Evelyn. She was his daughter, not his best friend. Well, yes, she was his truest friend, but not his best friend.

He looked at Stan. He was going to get an earful during his afternoon walk.

"I think you should go for it." Harper stood in front of him, where he read, for the second time, Evelyn's chapter.

"Is that Evelyn's?"

He shut the screen. "Yes."

He didn't want to lie. Besides, Stan was a terrible conversationalist. Maybe Harper could give him the female perspective. "Is it weird if I ask for dating advice from my daughter?"

She shrugged. "I think she's perfect. Seriously. Like, she's your perfect match."

"We should set up a section of beach reads."

"You should do a showcase of her books for the summer."

"No," he said. He wasn't going to budge on this. No matter how he felt about her, he wasn't going to sell Evelyn Rose romances. Ever.

"Why not?"

"Harps, don't ask. You're wasting your time." He still had some boundaries.

By lunch, Evelyn still hadn't responded. And he'd completely forgotten his mantra.

Mateo came walking through the front door to the store, and Charlie noticed Harper pop up from her chair and stuff a book back on its shelf. Harper had created a display of "Ask What We're Reading" with silly selfies of them in front of their book of the week. The problem was, Harper used this form of marketing as her duty while on the job. She was always reading her pick of the week.

"How's the house?" Harper asked Mateo.

"Older than I thought, but cool." He gave a nod to Charlie. "Mr. Maron."

"How are you doing, Mateo?"

"Good, Mr. Maron. You?"

He liked the young man that seemed smitten with Harper. He wasn't exactly sure what Harper's feelings were for Mateo, but whatever the reason, they didn't seem to go for it. At least, not to his knowledge.

Mateo handed Harper back the book she had lent him—a weekly tradition the two had started over a year ago. Harper would pick a book that had been sitting on the shelves for years and make him read it. Mateo would do as he was told and return for the next one. He'd stay for a coffee; she'd ask what he thought. He'd tell her. The awkwardness would continue until the end of the questioning. She'd give him the next book and promised that he'd love it; he would promise that he would. And the cycle would go on.

This was his cue for his walk. He'd take Stan along the beach.

Walks had been a way to clear his mind from the worries and stresses of the store. But this afternoon, his thoughts seemed to be like a pinball machine bouncing from one thought to the next. Evelyn's silence to Mateo working on Evelyn's house. He'd make a pretty penny from the job, but it would also be a test for all the other homeowners or soon-to-be owners on Martha's Vineyard. Finding a local contractor, one who understood the strange politics of small towns and rules and regulations that changed like the wind's direction, would be helpful for those trying to do some work on their island beach homes.

He'd set out for the beach, and even though he hadn't set out for the beach house, he found himself in front of it, staring at what might be a possibility.

Funny how he felt younger, eager for the time to pass. He hadn't wished time to pass in a long time or woken up excited about what the day might bring. The highs never came without the lows, and he expected that if things were to continue, it would be a very dark low. Much worse than the lows from when he'd first lost Evelyn.

Could he really lose her twice?

Could Harper be right, though? Maybe they were good together, and this reunion was more than just luck. Maybe they were meant to find each other again. God knew he needed something. He sat down on the sand, facing the water, Stan sitting next to him. He pulled out a notebook he had tucked away in a side table in his den. He opened to the last page he'd written. Almost seven years ago, he wrote seven words.

I have nothing inside me to write.

He had just celebrated his birthday—his fiftieth—with Harper, who had just turned twenty-one. Harper had been born one day before his birthday, and each year, they celebrated together—except that year. Her friends had taken her to the city, and she spent the weekend away.

He had encouraged her to go, not thinking twice about it until he realized no one had called. His parents had been dead. Martha hadn't remembered in years. His cousins had forgotten. The regulars hadn't stopped in the bookstore. That night, he'd sat with Stan, alone. His usually tiny home had felt big, too big for just him.

He hadn't written a full novel for a few years at that point, but he had picked up the notebook, just like he was doing now, and tried to write.

Nothing.

"Just can't get out of my own way," he said to Stan, shutting the notebook. He watched as the waves smashed into the cliffs. "Harper's going to get married someday, and it's going to be just you and me."

He had been dreading that day for so many years. He knew he had it good, that the past few years had been a gift. Most parents saw their child off sooner than twenty-eight. He just wished it could last forever.

He pulled out his phone and took a picture of the water and sent it to Evelyn with a caption. **Your view.**

The dots scattered against the bottom but dropped again.

His stomach dropped with them, triggering his doubt and insecurities. He opened the pages to his notebook again and wrote the date.

His phone vibrated in his pocket, and he dropped his pen and checked his phone.

You should sit on my deck and write.

He looked behind him. Her house sat back about a hundred yards from the water, tucked inside the valley, nestled among seagrass and wild rose bushes. He stood, wiping the sand off himself and leading Stan up the steps and down her walkway, all the way to her deck. The house had a wicker lounge chair that had seen better days. He let go of Stan's leash, and he lay down in the sun, stretching out his legs, his belly exposed.

He took another picture of the view and sent it to Evelyn.

Taking your advice.

He opened the notebook again. He stared at the empty lines, the daunting clean page. Holding the pen just above the paper, he did what she had suggested years ago.

Just write. Don't think about it, just do it.

So, he did.

And stopped.

And started again, scribbled out the words, ripped out the page, and started.

He wrote the date.

Then wrote *One* on top. And stared out at the water. He closed his eyes and took in a breath.

"Let your connection to the water guide your pace," Evelyn had said to him that first summer they met. Even then, writer's block was a real thing for him. "Push the words out with the waves."

They both shared the love of writing, but they were yin and yang when it came to styles, approaches, techniques, and everything else. She plotted, planned, and prepared. He dove right into something without knowing where the story was going. She studied other authors, genres, took classes. He read. She needed to talk things out, work on a scene, go back and forth, write it multiple times. He wanted to write and finish it. He never looked back until his editors forced him to.

He pressed the tip of his pen to the paper. He listened for the waves. At first, the wind and a car passing by obstructed the other sounds. But then he heard the first wave, like a pulse coming to, and he wrote his first sentence. Then he heard the second, and he wrote a second line, trying not to stop, even though he was sure whatever he was writing was garbage and he should just start over.

He heard the third and pushed to write something, anything that came to mind. Then the fourth. He almost picked up the pen, when another car drove by, blocking out the waves, but it left just in time for the next one. Then the fifth. And soon, he lost track of the waves. Like a machine that needed to be oiled, he had a rough start, but the next time he looked at his phone, he had pages of scribbles, notes, plans, timelines, character arcs, and had started a dreaded outline.

He shook out his hand and leaned back. Taking out his phone again, he snapped another photo, this time of his scribblings, then sent it to Evelyn.

I've taken your advice and worked on an outline.

The dots flashed across the bottom.

Can't wait to hear you read it at the next writer's group.

He had less than a week to get it into some sort of shape.

Then another text came through. **Can't wait to see you tomorrow.**

A current ran through his body, an invisible swell inside his chest.

He was falling in love again.

CHAPTER 17

"*Y*ou're holding out on me," Bitty said as Evelyn texted on her phone.

"What?" Evelyn pretended not to know what she was talking about. She stuffed her phone back into her purse.

"You heard me," Bitty said. Not repeating her statement. Not entertaining the dodge. "You said nothing was going on between the two of you, but you were canoodling on the bench this morning, you had an intimate moment after dinner last night, and now he's texting you all day. Let's hear the truth."

"I wasn't canoodling."

Bitty lifted her eyebrows. "You two sat close and intimate. Now spill it."

"It's complicated."

"And?"

"And he broke my heart, and I'm worried that these feelings are just old memories that should be left in the past."

"How did he break your heart?" Bitty asked. "What happened?"

The story was so long that it would take over a hundred novels to write about it.

"I let him go." It had been more complicated, more dramatic at the time. Her staying behind in Boston. Him leaving for Hollywood. The two of them agreed to pause the engagement. She'd known it was over the second he'd gotten on that plane. Not when he had called her excited about his new opportunities, new people, and so many more possibilities. She never would've thought the worst, though. That her best friend would swoop in when she turned her back.

Tanya had been her roommate at The Wharf every summer since she started working there, so when she heard they started a relationship, Evelyn had crumbled apart. The love of her life moved on with her best friend. Had they been together before? It had only been six months since they had broken up. It could've been sixty years as far as she'd been concerned. The two of them had betrayed her more severely than she could have ever imagined.

Then it was over. Her friendship, her relationship, everything.

She thought her life was over and then she met George.

She shook her memories away, but she couldn't shake the feeling that she was at the end of a road and she needed to choose the right path. Buying the house, helping Wanda, being open to Charlie—was this her path?

"What the heck am I doing?" Evelyn said.

She really wasn't asking Bitty, but when her friend, who now felt more like a sister, began to answer, she listened with her whole heart.

"Isn't it about taking one day at a time?" Her southern drawl drew out the word time.

Time.

If she had been given more time with George, she wouldn't have sat in the house worried about trivial things. She would've bought that beach house and taken that vacation. She would have encouraged her daughters to stay longer, visit more, and go to them. She wouldn't give space but get close, spend time, and live in the moment.

How much time did her life offer? It certainly wasn't endless.

The ocean, the sand, the cliffs, probably even her new home, will survive her. So, what did today offer?

They reached the hospital in just over an hour and parked in the hospital's garage. Charlie had texted twice, but she discouraged herself from replying in front of Bitty. She'd wait until she had somewhere private to write how she felt, freely, without peering eyes. She wanted to be open and honest, but should she dive right into something? She had just purchased the house. She was taking on the role of caretaker. She promised to be a mentor for a young writer. Should she enter a relationship too?

They stepped into Wanda's room, where she sat in bed, dressed in yoga pants and an oversized fleece. She looked drained; the color lost from her cheeks. When she saw them walk into the room, her eyes sparkled. "Girls, you came."

"Of course we came." Evelyn smiled, but she understood Wanda's apprehension. Her own husband had left her when the going got tough.

"How are you feeling?" Bitty asked her.

"Fine. Okay."

"Well, you look great," Bitty said, and Evelyn remembered her goal of bringing hope. The truth was, Wanda didn't look well. Dark bags hung under her eyes. Her cheekbones seemed harder along her jawline. Her glow relinquished, replaced with a paleness created by an evil illness.

"You're as beautiful as always." Evelyn put on a smile. Hope. She was giving her hope.

"What's the plan?" Wanda asked. "I called my neighbors, Kay and Walt, and told them I'd be staying for at least eight weeks."

The doctor explained they would start with at least four-to-eight rounds of chemotherapy, then move on to hormone therapy. Their hopes were to manage the cancer and kill it. Every three weeks, she'd need to travel to Boston General and receive her chemotherapy treatments. Then she could go back to the island and have her check-ups through the local general practitioner, who also worked at Boston General once a week.

"You have an appointment with your new oncologist tomorrow," Bitty said. "I also set up that facial we were talking about."

"That's nice of you to set up all those things for me." Wanda's eyes moistened. "I can't thank you ladies enough."

Evelyn didn't want to get emotional. Not because she didn't feel as emotional as Wanda, but she wanted to stay levelheaded for her friend. She wanted to be the eyes and ears for Wanda when the doctors and nurses gave information. She wanted to be able to get through this for Wanda's sake, not her own. Wanda had to deal with living with breast cancer. Evelyn had a responsibility to her new friend, and she took that with great respect.

She then thought about Charlie. What was she thinking? She couldn't get involved with someone right now. She didn't have time to date.

The doctors came in to give final orders and prescriptions. Wanda went home with a litany of medications.

Just as she silenced her phone from Charlie's third text, a clunk came from the window, where a pigeon landed on the sill. It flapped its wings, hitting the window again, its eyes looking in as if staring at Evelyn.

She looked around to see if anyone had noticed, but Bitty and Wanda had begun the process of signing all the discharge papers. The pigeon didn't move from the sill but kept its eyes on Evelyn. A warmth filled her soul, and the emotions she held back came rushing up to her chest.

Okay, George. I'll keep flying, she said in her head.

She peeked at Charlie's text and texted back. Her stomach churned like a whirlpool as she hit send. What would he think?

He sent back a picture of her view from the house.

It was gorgeous.

She watched as the pigeon flew away.

CHAPTER 18

*E*velyn wrote all night. She sat on the couch, her computer screen the only light in the room. She opened the sliding glass doors and let the waves and scent enter her space. She hadn't written this madly in a long, long time. Even before George's passing, years before. Her fingers blazed against the keys. One thousand within a half hour, two within an hour. By six AM, she had three and a half thousand words. She was flying.

She grabbed her pocketbook to meet Bitty at Wanda's room, when her room's phone rang. Only Charlie had rung the hotel's room. Her heart sped up as she grabbed the phone.

"Hello?" she said into the receiver.

"You're alive," her sister Carol said.

Her heart stopped. "Yes."

Carol sounded annoyed. "I've been calling all night."

Evelyn looked at her phone. She must've missed Carol's messages.

"I'm sorry. I went into the city."

"I thought you were relaxing on the island." Carol sighed. "Well, I'm glad you're okay. Are you at least having fun?"

"You were right, Carol," Evelyn said. "This was the best thing I could've done for myself."

"Really?" Carol's voice lifted. "Are you serious? Or are you just being sarcastic?"

"I'm serious." Evelyn didn't know if Carol would think she had lost her mind, but she had nothing to lose at this point. "I haven't told the girls, so don't spill the beans, but I bought a beach house."

"What?" Carol practically yelled into the phone. "You bought a beach house?"

She laughed at her sister's dramatics. "Yes. A gorgeous Victorian gambrel with dormers and a wraparound porch and the most amazing view of the ocean."

"That's wonderful!" Carol sounded happy for her. "But you haven't told the girls?"

"I haven't had time." That wasn't true. She had called both girls yesterday before she went to sleep, but they didn't pick up. Renee texted something about having work, and she'd call when she could. Her daughter ran a restaurant with her husband in Chicago and worked all the time. Samantha was abroad in London under the guise of fashion, but she visited castles and drank in pubs mostly and posted everything on social media.

But when would she tell them about the house? About Wanda and Bitty? About Charlie?

Harper seemed to know everything about Charlie, even alluded to knowing about the fallout between Evelyn and Charlie and Tanya's involvement. Her daughters didn't even know Charlie existed.

"I'd love for you to visit," she offered.

"I wish I could, but I don't have time." Carol started in her spiel of how busy her life was with sports. "All I do is drive teenagers around. I'm like their butler. I wish I could come to Martha's Vineyard."

"Think about it." Evelyn wanted to remind her sister to slow down and see how lucky she was, but Carol didn't need reminding. It had been the old Evelyn that needed the reminding.

"I can't believe you bought a beach house." Carol did sound genuinely delighted for Evelyn. "I told you the trip was a good idea."

"It needs some work, but it's mine."

The house was hers.

She promised to call Carol after she talked to the girls and left to meet the ladies.

They stayed that morning, sitting on Wanda's deck with scones, coffee, and some fruit. Wanda didn't eat much. It always worried Evelyn when someone didn't eat much. The stomach spoke volumes about someone's well-being.

"What are our plans?" Bitty had her phone out and had created a shared calendar for the three women. "We should figure out the rest of this week and into next week. I've canceled my flight back to Oklahoma. I can't believe it's already been a whole week already."

"I extended our hotel rooms for another week." Evelyn had to do a lot of negotiating and made special arrangements in order to get the rooms they were staying in, but with an offer of extra cash, the hotel had been more than happy to accommodate.

"I can't have you pay for our rooms," Wanda said.

But Evelyn wasn't having it. So, she changed the subject.

"Wanda has treatment every third Tuesday." Evelyn looked at her own phone, where she had typed in some notes from the hospital. "We can catch the seven A.M. ferry to make it to her infusion."

Wanda had shown nothing but gratitude and strength and perseverance over these past few days, but Evelyn couldn't help but worry how Wanda was dealing with everything. The doctor had recommended making lists and arrangements for everything, having back-up plans in case things changed, and going over the plan frequently.

"It makes the patient feel a sense of control," he'd told her.

He had also recommended therapy, which Evelyn hadn't booked. She didn't know Wanda well enough to know if it would insult her by making an appointment or not. She was about to bring it up, when Wanda closed her eyes.

"You okay, Wanda?" Evelyn asked, sitting up in her chair to get a better angle of Wanda's face.

"I didn't sleep well, I'm afraid." Her eyes opened and looked out at the water. "I called Bill and let him know I was staying in Martha's Vineyard and continuing my treatments here." Wanda's eyes dropped to her hands. "He wished me well."

"Ah, honey, I'm really sorry," Bitty said, reaching out and squeezing her hand.

Wanda's eyes didn't show emotion. If anything, they showed nothing.

But Evelyn was the hypocrite, suggesting Wanda talk about death. How many times had the girls asked her to see someone? Or Carol? Or Sue?

"I was thinking of setting up a session with a therapist," Evelyn said. "I've never really dealt with losing George." Evelyn had tried for so long on her own, but maybe it was time to talk to someone about everything. "Have you thought about talking to someone about Bill and about being sick?"

Wanda played with a ring on her finger. "No. I guess that wouldn't be such a bad idea."

"I talked to my pastor after Richard," Bitty said. "It was more about talking and letting it all out."

"I believe . . ." Evelyn began to say. "I believe something, maybe it's a greater power or maybe it's fate or maybe it's just plain coincidence, but *something* brought us together, so we don't have to worry about those who left anymore."

Bitty grinned. "A sisterhood."

A little spark flickered back into Wanda's eyes. "A sisterhood."

When she left the hotel to meet with Mateo at the house, she bumped into Mitch in the hotel lobby with his luggage. He was checking out. A week had gone by so fast, yet so much had happened in a course of seven days.

"Hey, you," he said. She couldn't hold back her smile at his audacity. He still couldn't remember her name. "You finally got rid of Wanda."

The joke hit her in the stomach, and she became embarrassed at her behavior. She was about to turn away, but she said, "Are you headed out?"

He nodded, patting his carry-on bag hanging off his shoulder.

"That's too bad," she said. "I was hoping to get to know you better."

"Are you staying longer?" He looked at his phone. "My flight doesn't leave until tonight."

"Save me a seat, would you? On the ferry?" she asked. "I'm just finishing up a few last-minute items and will be on the ferry in no time. I'd love a coffee with cream."

He snapped his fingers and pointed at her. "Coffee with cream."

She laughed to herself as she watched Mitch hurry off to the ferry. She imagined him getting in line, waiting for her to come.

For the rest of the day, Evelyn's schedule was full. She signed papers with the real estate agent, faxed her attorney more contracts and deeds, and talked on and off with her bank so many times she lost count. Then she had an idea.

"Good afternoon, Martha's Mysteries, how can I help you?" Harper said on the line.

"Harper?" she said. "It's Evelyn."

"Evelyn!" Harper immediately started talking about her writing. How she had written all night. How she was waiting on pins and needles for the agent to read her chapters. How she hadn't slept in days because of the excitement. "I can't wait to share with the group. You're coming back, right?"

"Harper, do you know anyone looking for some side work? Maybe willing to be an assistant? Run errands, do odd jobs here and there, wait for deliveries—things like that?"

"Uh, yeah. Me," Harper said.

It was exactly what Evelyn had hoped for. "Really? You have the time?"

"What do you need?" she asked.

Evelyn thought about the hours and the pay. She already had her assistant back home. Donna would be able to handle old Evelyn Rose stuff, while Harper could handle the new Evelyn stuff. "I'm looking for a few hours daily, but I'm flexible. I need someone willing to run to the pharmacy or on other errands for me, but who's also willing to wait around for deliveries if I'm unavailable. Someone who can answer emails, fill out paperwork, and do other little odds and ends. Just for the summer."

"Sounds perfect." Harper sounded eager. "I'd love to help."

"I'll need you as soon as tomorrow," Evelyn said, hoping this wouldn't change things. The exchange of deeds happened sooner than she expected. The Buckley's great niece was more than happy to sell the family beach house from San Diego.

"I'm closing on the house at the bank and need someone to wait for the furniture delivery."

"I can be there," she said with no hesitation.

Relief washed over Evelyn. "Thank you, Harper."

"No problem." Her voice was chirpy. "I'll see you tomorrow. Have fun with my dad tonight."

Evelyn hadn't forgotten about tonight. Dinner with Charlie had been stuck in her mind all day.

CHAPTER 19

*C*harlie hadn't been this nervous in a long time. Dinner was in less than two hours. Harper had an outfit laid out for him, ready to wear, but it looked tight and stiff. And like a child not wanting to wear their Sunday best, he felt a tantrum coming on.

"Really, Harper, a black tie?" he said, shouting to the kitchen from his bedroom.

"It's going to be so romantic." She poked her head into the room.

"But this isn't me," he said, dropping the tie and grabbing the dinner jacket.

"Exactly. You're showing her you'd do anything for her." She clasped her hands together and rested them against her chest. "You're a handsome old man and still pretty fit."

"Are you complimenting me?"

"You'll look great." She put the tie back on top of the hanger. "You're going to show her the time of her life tonight. I have everything all set."

He groaned. Harper had taken the liberty of making this into a romantic comedy scene.

"I don't stay up past ten o'clock most nights. Let's be real." He sat on the bed. "I think this is a mistake."

"What?" Harper rushed at him. "You two are perfect for—"

"Friends," he cut her off. "We're perfect for being friends." He waited to continue until she stopped playing with his hair. But when she didn't, he took her hand and removed it from his head. "Evelyn just lost her husband. She's taking care of her friend, who is sick. She's in no position to start dating, especially with our history."

"What did you do?" Harper asked for the millionth time, her eyes accusatory. "I know you were the reason you two didn't make it."

"Why do you assume it was all my fault?' he asked.

"Then it was Mom's."

He wished so many things at that moment. He wished he could lay out how he really felt. Yes, it was her mother. But, yes, he messed up too. He broke Evelyn's trust and heart in one fell swoop. He lost her after Tanya. But the truth was, he lost her before Tanya.

"Look, leave your mother out of this," he reminded her. "She's made her own messes, but none of mine."

"Me, being one of those messes," she said.

Harper never could fully forgive Tanya leaving her. He had years ago, because he had been grateful, she had left. Sure, it had been hard, but they had been miserable together, and dragging a child through that would have destroyed Harper. She had been so young when they divorced; he wondered if she could even remember them together.

"You're the best thing that ever happened to me. I wouldn't change a thing in my life. Not one thing." He paused to let it sink in. "I'm glad Evelyn's back in town, but you're still the most important thing to me."

Harper rolled her eyes. "So, you're not going to tell me what happened between the two of you?"

"No, I'm not going to tell you," Charlies said.

"Nobody is saying you have to marry Evelyn." Harper spoke to him as if he were a child.

"Thanks. I was saving up for a ring," he teased, trying to lighten the mood.

Harper put her hand on his shoulder. "You have a second chance that romance novels are made of." She picked up the jacket. "Now go and knock her socks off."

He moaned, then grabbed the outfit that had been perfectly placed on the hanger and was being held out by Harper. "I'm not wearing the tie."

After he showered, shaved, and shot back a quick swig of whiskey, he was off. He was glad the night air had cooled from the humid afternoon as he walked to The Wharf. Luckily, he wasn't driving, because he was sure to have another shot before he went to her suite to pick her up. He hadn't been this nervous since the first time he took her on a date.

When he stepped into the hotel, memories rushed like tidal waves washing over him. So many memories. How could those couple of years with Evelyn have so many when the last few had so little? He could place himself in vivid scenes with her, details alive in his head, but he couldn't remember what he'd done a week ago.

He walked past the lobby, when he saw Bitty sitting with the woman from the bookstore that first time with Evelyn. She waved and he decided to say hello.

The petite-framed Wanda looked like a child from behind. Crouched in the chair, she looked small and delicate, as if she could break. She smiled as he approached. He could see Bitty saying something to her, which made her beauty cover her illness for a split second, but he could see in her pale face that she was sick.

"Bitty," he said cheerily, embracing her in a hug as she stood. He turned to the woman still seated. "You must be Wanda. We sort of met at the bookstore."

"Yes, I remember." Wanda reached out her hand, and he took

it into his. It was limp, cold. He took his other and rubbed it gently.

"It's a pleasure," he said.

Wanda's eyes sparkled, and he could feel a squeeze back at him. "Yes, a pleasure."

Bitty winked at him as he let go of Wanda's hand. "You here for our girl?"

He nodded, holding out the flowers and gift he'd brought. Harper insisted he bring chocolates from the local fudge shop, but he thought of something better. Something he knew she liked. "I was just about to head up." He gestured toward the elevators. "You ladies have a lovely night."

By the time he reached her room, he could feel beads of sweat forming on his forehead. He silently prayed to himself to not let the night be a disaster. But then, disaster seemed to follow him.

"You're here," she said, swinging open the door before he had a chance to knock.

Her hair blew back behind her shoulders as the door swung open.

"You look fantastic," he said suddenly.

She blushed as she stood on the threshold in a sundress that fit her perfectly. "Thank you. You look great too."

He wanted to undo his top button, but instead, he handed over the flowers. "These are for you."

She sniffed the lilies from his garden. "They're beautiful."

She opened the door and let him in. The suite opened to a sitting room with a wall of windows from floor to ceiling and an unobstructed view of the Atlantic. It was as if they were floating on top of the water.

"This is incredible." He moved deeper into the room, which he quickly realized was a luxury suite. He knew she had a very successful career but was surprised she could buy a God-knows-how-much house on the Vineyard Sound while staying in a suite with a living room, dining room, and what looked like a private

Jacuzzi running the length of the patio that faced the Atlantic Ocean.

"Yes, it's very nice," she said, gesturing to him to sit before folding her hands together. "Would you like something to drink?"

"Do you have something to kill my nerves?" he joked, hoping to lighten the mood.

She smiled. "I have a white wine chilling in the fridge. Does that work?"

"That's perfect."

He walked around the sitting area, checking out the view. "All those years working here, and I never came up here. It's gorgeous."

"I came up a few times when I worked room service." She pulled out the cork. "But it didn't look like this."

"How much does this kind of upgrade cost you? Or did it come with your trip's package?" He was curious but then realized how rude he sounded. He shook his hands out in front of him. "Please allow me to apologize for being so nosy."

She poured the wine into glasses. "It's fine."

He took the glass but noticed she didn't answer the question. It had to have been a mighty big upgrade.

"Would you like to sit out on the balcony?" she asked, sliding open the floor-to-ceiling doors, the kind that folded into themselves.

"That sounds perfect."

She picked up a tray of food and his drink, and he followed her out to the table set up under an awning.

"The view is gorgeous." The Wharf sat right on the water, although it didn't have the cliffs or the sand dunes her new house had. It had concrete and asphalt surrounding it. The hotel's beach was small, whereas one felt small at Sugar Beach.

The waves rolled into the shore calmly, not helping to mute the silence that grew between them.

He then handed her the gift he'd brought. "This is for you."

She smiled and he could feel the ground moving underneath

him. Emotions stirred inside him like the sediment on the bottom of the ocean floor, tumbling around, unable to control itself. Carefully, she removed the wrapping paper.

"This is gorgeous." She put the leather-bound journal up to her face and inhaled. "Where did you get this?"

It hadn't come from a store. "I made it."

He had been playing around with other hobbies with his writer's block. Woodworking, art, glassblowing, pottery . . .

"I sell them in the store." He looked away, feeling foolish in the grand suite that cost more than what he made from his silly little hobby.

"I love it." She took her thumb and leafed through the pages, studying the stitching. "Do you make art journals? Or recipe books? I'd love to get some for my daughters."

"Are your daughters still in Minnesota?" he asked.

She shook her head. "My oldest, Renee, lives in Chicago with her husband. They just got married a few years ago, and my youngest is traveling abroad in Europe, working for a fashion blog."

"That sounds glamorous," he said.

She let out a breath. "Yes, she likes it."

There was something about the way she looked off, or maybe it was the way her shoulders had lowered a bit, but he could tell that her daughters were a touchy subject.

"How's the writing?" he asked, bringing up the one subject he had wanted to avoid.

"I'm still struggling." This time, she sighed loudly. She sat closer in her chair with him, and he knew this was what she wanted to talk to him about.

"What's the issue?" he asked.

"I've never written without knowing the ending."

That sounded like every novel and every screenplay he had ever written. "It's like driving in the fog. You never really know what's coming until you're close enough. You have to rely on instinct."

"It's frustrating." She sipped her wine.

"You'll get there," he assured her. "You just have to let go and let the story take you there."

"I'm afraid of what might happen to my character," she answered.

"You of all people should know what it's like to kill off your darlings." It came out before he could stop himself, and he cringed as he waited for her reaction.

She looked at him. He didn't know what had made him say it. He didn't care. He didn't need to know why the character she had killed off, the character that had been so obviously based on him, had to die.

She made a second sigh, and at this point, he felt like a fool. "Please, I didn't mean to . . ."

He stopped himself. Maybe he had.

She crossed her leg, holding her knee with both hands. "I should apologize, I guess, for killing your character."

"I never cheated." He said it quickly—before he could regret it.

The series had started off with the heroine's fiancé dying in a car accident while coming home from a night with his mistress. That was what bothered him. Not only had she killed him but he was also a cheater.

"You didn't need to sleep with Tanya to cheat." She moved positions in her chair. "You two hung out together all the time. Every time I called, you were together."

When he'd arrived in Hollywood, he'd been completely lost. The screenplay was being reworked, rewritten, and revised so much that it hardly looked like his original novel, which he'd signed his rights away. He'd floundered in Los Angeles. The city had been too crowded. He could hardly afford rent. The executives hadn't listened to him. His writing had turned scripted, forced, and full of foolishness he hated in big motion pictures.

The movie kept getting hit with "red tape," but the studio had hired him as a writer for a series show on primetime. When he'd talked to Evelyn, her anxieties of him being taken advantage, of being used and discarded, of being broken by the machine that was Hollywood, made him keep quiet. He hadn't wanted to disappoint her by being the fool she worried he would become.

When Tanya kept calling him, it had been nice to have someone familiar in Los Angeles to introduce him to people. He had enjoyed seeing a familiar face in the sea of fakes. But when she noticed how miserable he was, she asked him to tell her the truth. He had confessed everything and it felt good. She hadn't told him he was a fool or that he should've listened to Evelyn and stayed behind. She had encouraged him to keep going, to work on this project to get to the next. She told him he could do it, and in that moment, he needed someone, anyone, on his side.

"I never cheated," he said again.

She looked away. "I guess it was easier to think you did, because you just falling out of love with me felt much worse."

"Evelyn." He shifted in his seat to face her. He wanted to laugh. "I never fell out of love with you. I'm still crazy about you."

He grabbed hold of her hand, and she didn't remove it.

"I've dreamt of this moment for the past thirty years," he said, placing his other hand on top, holding her eyes with his. "I have never stopped loving you."

She bit her bottom lip, then placed her hand on top of his. "I guess that makes two of us, because I'm not sure if I ever stopped loving you."

Without another moment of hesitation, Charlie leaned over and kissed Evelyn on the lips.

CHAPTER 20

$\mathcal{I}$t would take officially five days for the bank to send the money for the sale of the house, but the Buckley's took Evelyn's down payment as enough good faith to allow her to move in.

The day after her night with Charlie, she met Harper at the house with the journal he had given her. The furniture delivery would be arriving that morning, and she had a plumber coming out as well as Mateo. Things suddenly became very real and very expensive. But all she could think about throughout the day was the kiss she'd shared with Charlie.

That kiss had been everything she had been hoping for since she saw him at the bookstore. That kiss had passion—so much passion that her toes curled thinking about it. That kiss had flipped her stomach and her head upside down. That kiss got her writing again. She hadn't written so much, so fast in too long. The words had literally poured out of her.

"It looks like the plumbing hasn't been updated for at least sixty years. Maybe more,"

Phil, the plumber said. "It's gonna cost you."

Her stomach flipped again, not by the cost, but by the image of Charlie's hand holding hers.

"Replace it all if you have to. I want this place to be standing for another sixty years."

Phil narrowed his eyes as if suspicious. "I'm going to have to remove some of the floors, especially the bathrooms, it's going to take weeks to do it right."

The plumber seemed to be dragging his feet about the job.

"I give you permission to do whatever it takes."

"I have another job over on the other side of the island," he said.

"Mateo had said you were available." She stared at the overweight middle-aged man, whose story had suddenly changed when he'd met her with no Mr. Rose.

"I may run over my estimate, depending on the market." Phil stood there as if there was something else he wanted to say, but he hesitated.

"But . . ?" She waited for his next excuse.

"Are you sure you want me to stay with this timeline? I'll have to start ordering all the supplies and parts. I'll also have to hire a few guys to help with the labor."

She wondered if he would be this hesitant if she were a man asking for the work. Would he hold his judgment like he seemed to be questioning hers? She pulled out her checkbook and wrote out a generous down payment, double what he asked for.

"Is there a problem?" she asked, ripping the check off the book at its perforated edges and handing it over to him.

He looked down at the amount and whistled. "None whatsoever."

She squeezed her jaw, holding back the thrill that swept through her. She shook his hand, but a bit firmer than when she had first greeted him. As she walked through the front door, *her front door*, she stopped and looked out. She was about to step over a whole new threshold, start a whole new story with a whole new self to discover.

She walked in.

She didn't close the door but left it open, letting the light come in. A glass door would be perfect there. Her fingers tapped the wooden spindles as she walked by the staircase into the kitchen, which was at the back end of the house. She wanted this house to be nothing but light. Walls and halls and bedrooms full of light and views. She wanted to be able to stand in every room of the house and have a view of the sea.

Sea View.

That's what she would call her house.

"Harper," she said as the young woman walked through the house. "I'd like you to order me a sign for above the front door. Like this."

She held up an image she'd found on Pinterest. "I want to name the house, Sea View."

"That's perfect," Harper said.

Evelyn hadn't spent too much time with Harper, but the young lady was pure sunshine and happiness.

"Would you like to stay for dinner, and we can talk more about your story?"

Harper grimaced. "I totally would, but I just made plans with Mateo."

She jabbed her thumb at the young contractor who worked on measurements with two other men.

"You know what? He'll totally understand." Harper went to walk away, but Evelyn stopped her.

"No, that's silly. We can get together another night. I'll be living here, after all." Evelyn laughed at the thought. She lived on Martha's Vineyard. She was sticking around.

She then stretched her neck at Mateo. "You two would be cute together."

Harper's cheeks blushed pink. "We're just friends. He's really busy with his business and I'm busy with writing."

"What if I had everyone over for dinner tomorrow?"

When she and George first got married, Evelyn had loved throwing dinner parties. As it turned out, working at The Wharf all those summers had made her a great doctor's wife. She could prepare a few good meals, set a beautiful table, and have great drinks ready to be served.

She would invite Charlie and the girls. It would be fun to include Harper and Mateo, as well. Maybe even Phil. "Why don't you and Mateo come? I'll invite your father. I'll have my girlfriends—" She stopped when she noticed Harper's face. "Or is that weird?"

"I think dinner sounds like a wonderful idea." Harper clasped her hands together, then immediately went in for a hug. Evelyn stiffened, but as Harper held on, she leaned into it. "This is going to be fun."

They went through a menu and created a list of groceries and supplies for the feast. Harper skipped away to run the errands, and left Evelyn feeling a tug. She missed her own daughters.

She picked up her phone and called Renee.

"Hey," Renee said, picking up on the fourth ring. "I can explain."

"What if I was dead in a ditch?" Evelyn said dramatically, trying to sound as if it were a joke, but just like that the old Evelyn, the one driven by fear came out. Renee had avoided her calls for weeks now.

"I'm sorry." Renee tended to disappear on Evelyn. Weeks would go by and nothing. No word. No texts. No calls. Not even enough space on her dang voicemail to leave a message.

Text after text, Evelyn would send, but nothing.

Once, she had asked for a daily "proof of life" pic, but she never followed through. Then George died and it got worse.

"Please just give me peace of mind," Evelyn pleaded, trying not to sound like the nagging mother she knew her daughter thought she was.

"I'm busy, and an adult."

"You're my daughter. Who lives in downtown Chicago. Who works in a restaurant until two in the morning. I get worried when you don't let me know if you're alive."

"Mom." Her voice was flat.

"Yes?"

"Are you just calling me to give me a hard time?"

Evelyn did sound naggy. "No, I'm calling to let you know I bought a beach house."

"Where?" Renee asked, her voice almost disinterested.

"I've bought this Victorian." She waited for another reaction, but the line remained silent, so she continued. "On Martha's Vineyard. I want you and Harry to come stay. I'll fly you all out to vacation."

"I'm super busy in the summer. I can't just fly to Martha's Vineyard." Renee sounded annoyed at the invitation. Evelyn clenched her jaw. Her daughter worked hard. That's a trait she got from Evelyn. George would tease that they were two peas in a pod. Same strange organizational skills and then oddly creative, but they were both stubborn and hard to break. Her teenage years had created deep divots between their once-close relationship. Now they had half the country in between them.

"It's an open invitation. Let me know when you'd like to come, and I'll get everything together for you guys."

"Have you talked to Samantha?" Renee changed the subject.

"Not recently, but she calls me back," Evelyn threw in.

She wondered where things had fallen apart. She hadn't really explored any of those feelings and thoughts. Was it her? Had they escaped her? Or had they escaped the pain of George's death like she had? And was it too late to get back what they had? Or had that died as well?

"Come," Evelyn said again. "It's gorgeous."

"I have a ton of stuff that needs to get done," Renee said.

"Well, think about it." Evelyn gave up and thought about the sea glass tumbling on the bottom of the ocean floor, smoothing itself out by allowing it to be tumbled, not fighting every step of the way. "I love you."

"I love you too."

"I love you…" Evelyn said into the phone, silently waiting for the next part of their exchange.

"To the moon and back," Renee said, finishing their ritual.

Evelyn let out a sigh of relief. Evelyn worried about her the most. Renee held things inside, not letting many, if anyone, in. "Think about it."

"Okay, fine. If you'll leave me alone about it."

The line went silent. But Evelyn could tell Renee was still on the other end. With a bit of hesitation, Renee asked. "Are you . . . selling the house?"

Evelyn wasn't entirely sure, but she wanted to be honest. "I hired a real estate agent to see what I could get for it. If you want it, I can hold on to it. Rent it out to a family in the meantime."

"I wouldn't want you to have to do that," Renee said. The line went silent again. In fact, she hadn't expected Renee, out of the two girls, to care. She'd driven to Chicago to live in the city, had attended culinary school, and taken the first job she'd landed and never looked back.

"Think about coming to the island and about the house back home, okay?" Evelyn felt bad she had dumped all that on her eldest daughter, but if she wasn't going to call, then that's what happened in adulthood. "And call your mother back when she calls you."

"I will." Renee groaned. "I gotta go, Mom. I have to get ready for work."

"Okay, but—"

"I know. I'll think about it." She hung up after saying the fastest goodbye ever.

Evelyn stepped out onto the back deck where the Buckleys must've had barbeques and family dinners, listening for the crashing waves and the cries of seagulls. The tang of ocean air mixed in with the sun-toasted seagrass permeated around her.

She arranged the furniture as the delivery guys removed the old Buckley stuff. Most of it would be stored in the garage until Phil and Mateo finished the bedrooms. She watched as the rooms slowly transformed. She had bought a plush soft-blue sofa to off-set the leather chairs, a large area rug, and lots of throw pillows.

She wanted the house to feel as cozy and as comforting as possible. The living room would be the one space that didn't need work right away like the bathrooms, kitchen, and dining room.

The upstairs view was unparalleled to anything she had seen anywhere on the island. The space had three dormers that looked out at the water. She could see everything from the lighthouse and the cliffs to the tiny village of Eastport off in the east. The fine, sandy shore of Sugar Beach was in full view.

She imagined a sitting area where she could write in the morning, with a fireplace and a large picture window. She'd put in French doors and add a balcony. She'd add dormers on. the front side of the house and a bathroom with a tub with views of the hills and cliffs.

By midmorning, Harper arrived with all the supplies Evelyn had sent her for. Cleaning supplies, a vacuum, rags for cleaning, a few buckets, a mop, and more.

"Can you pick up this order tomorrow morning?" Evelyn asked, sending the pickup text to her from the hardware store. "I ordered a few basics for the house."

"You bet." The property came with a shed, a lawnmower, and a few other items for the yard, but she would need more simple things that George had always had on hand—a hammer, screwdrivers, a measuring tape, a plunger and so much more she probably had no idea about. There was a lot to do, but all the planning and lists of things she needed only made her more excited of the new adventure.

Her goal was to make Wanda and Bitty as comfortable as possible. She got the basics, and she'd need more, but she decided to wait to see what they needed.

What she splurged on right away was the outdoor furniture. She bought a long table capable of fitting twelve for the back deck. She also purchased an outdoor grill, along with one of those gas fire pits. A glass coffee table, along with heaters and a couple large umbrellas to sit under, a few Adirondack chairs and loungers for the back, and a swing for the front porch.

By evening, when the movers had left and Mateo and his workers had gone home, Evelyn walked through the house and turned on all the lights. She carried a box of lightbulbs, changing any that didn't work and putting them in the new lamps she had bought. Like a Thomas Kinkade, the house glowed.

She walked from room to room and floor to floor, then to the porch and onto the deck, listening, looking in, watching as the sun lowered in the sky—taking everything in.

This was her house.

This was her view.

This was her new life.

She texted the girls first.

Dinner tomorrow night by the ocean at our new summer house, Sea View.

Bitty sent a GIF of an old woman dancing a jig, making Evelyn laugh out loud. Wanda replied with a double pink heart. **Love the name!**

Just as she was about to reply, Phil cleared his throat.

The plumber stood at the edge of the deck with a clipboard in his hands. "I've ordered all the plumbing for the baths."

"And the third floor?" she asked.

"Including the third floor."

She smiled and let out a giggle that made her sound like a little kid opening her big present on Christmas.

"Great," she said and then laughed at herself.

"I'm happy to help restore this old place." Then she saw the gruff man smile back at her. They may have started out on the wrong foot, but he seemed like a nice enough guy.

"I'm having a dinner here tomorrow night," she began, "with some friends. You should come. Invite your wife or whoever."

She guessed he was about her age, maybe a bit older.

He looked surprised by the offer. "You want to invite your plumber to dinner?"

She laughed at his response. "Why not?"

She guessed George had never invited the handyman or the

landscaper over for dinner. But maybe they should have. Maybe she should've joined a community so when George did pass away, and the girls left for good, she wouldn't be so lonely and dependent on them.

"You know what? Sure," he said, putting a mechanical pencil behind his ear. "Can I bring anything besides potty jokes?"

"Just your jokes." she laughed. "I've invited some others from town, including Mateo."

Mateo had been the one who suggested hiring Phil, along with his brother, Elias, her new electrician, and a woman from town for interior design.

"Good kid, that Mateo," he said. "Let me at least bring my infamous salsa and chips."

"Salsa and chips would be great."

As she walked Phil out and opened the door, Charlie walked up the steps.

"Charlie." She froze, not expecting to see him. Her face immediately blushed. Could he tell she had been thinking of him all day?

"I hope you don't mind I stopped by," he said. He reached out his hand and said, "Phil, it's good to see you."

"Good to see you too."

"Phil's coming to dinner tomorrow night. Will you be joining us?" she asked.

Charlie made a slight face, but then said, "Sure. I'd love to join you and Phil."

Phil waved goodbye, and she stepped aside, waving him inside. "Come out back with me."

He hesitated. "Look, it's none of my business, but is there something going on with you and Phil?"

She laughed. Phil was not her type. She shook her head. "No, he's more interested in environmentally-friendly toilets than me."

"Does that make you sad?"

She laughed at his sudden jealousy. "No, it does not make me sad."

She reached out to grab his hand, but he stuffed it into his pocket and stepped away from her reach.

"You okay?"

"No, I'm not."

Her heart dropped. "What is it?"

He started to pace in the small space in the front hall. "I can't eat. I can't sleep. I can't think rationally."

He stopped in front of her. "I know you've lost George, and you have your girls, and you're starting this new life. And I want to be part of your life. I really do."

Her throat dried up as she waited for the *but*.

"But I can't just be friends." He started pacing again, dragging his fingers through his hair.

She smiled. "Good."

He stopped pacing. "I want it all. I want to be all in."

"Are you asking me to go steady?" she asked.

He didn't answer. Instead, he rushed to her, swooping her into his arms. He placed his hand behind her neck, tangling his fingers in her hair and bringing her lips to his. He kissed her passionately, longingly, as if he had waited thirty years to do so.

Her arms wrapped around his neck. Her eyes closed as she kissed him back.

Evelyn didn't stay at the hotel that night. She stayed up, sitting under the stars with Charlie on the house's deck. They made a fire and sat with blankets, listening to the crickets singing in sync with the waves. They talked and talked and talked.

"I talked to Hank about the origin of the house," he said. "He's a member of the historical society on the island."

"Does he know much about it?" She had intended to do a little digging herself at the closing with the Buckley's great-niece, who had overseen the sale.

"It was built in eighteen sixty-two by a US senator," he said.

She could see through the dirt and grime of the Victorian gambrel and see its charm and beauty. "My hope is to restore it, but also allow families to pass it down."

She hoped her own great-niece would be able to stay there one day. She took him through the house, telling him all her thoughts so far as they walked from room to room.

"When do you plan on moving in?" he asked.

"As soon as tomorrow." She had most of the furniture. A working bathroom upstairs and down, including the half bath. There were a total of four bedrooms, not including the attic on the third floor. Nothing was preventing her.

"Are Wanda and Bitty moving in as well?" he asked.

"Yes, that's the plan." Then she quickly added, "For at least the summer."

Would that change his mind? Would he tolerate dating a woman who was living like the Golden Girls?

At some point in the night, when the tide started going out, Charlie turned to her and said, "You want to go on a treasure hunt?"

She tilted her head, curious if she'd heard him right. "A treasure hunt now?"

He nodded. "I have a couple flashlights in the back of my truck. The beach is empty."

The Evelyn from a week ago would have scoffed at the idea. She'd be in bed, but not sleeping. She'd be waiting to wake up to do nothing. Again.

She leaned over and kissed him like she had been all night. "Yes. I'd love to go on a treasure hunt."

He kissed her long, holding her lips to his, pressing as though he didn't want to let go. When he left for the flashlights, she traced her lips with her fingertips and giggled to herself. She never in a million years would've thought she'd be back on Martha's Vineyard and in Charlie's arms.

She wrapped the blanket around herself, listening as the front door opened and shut. Then heard the crunching of the seashell driveway under his steps. The door of a truck. Then his heavy footsteps down the deck.

"Martha drew at least a dozen different renditions of what my grandfather told her."

He dropped a satchel on the floor, the smell of old leather filling the space as he opened it up, pulling out a journal. The smell brought her back to being a young woman with endless possibilities in front of her. She leaned in close to him, feeling his leg against hers and enjoying the electricity his touch sent throughout her body. He opened the journal to the middle—an ink drawing of dotted lines and what looked like the shoreline.

She pointed to a drawn X. "So it's there."

"Well, maybe. If this particular version is right."

"How many versions are there?"

Charlie handed her a flashlight. "At least a dozen or so."

He stood up and held out his hand. "You ready for an adventure?"

"Absolutely."

CHAPTER 21

*T*here had been no buried treasure, but Charlie had found treasure, nonetheless. Evelyn was everything. He didn't leave that night. Instead, he stayed up all night with her, watching as the stars disappeared, a pink glow coming up beyond the horizon. Silhouettes of swooping birds floated above the seagrass, waking up with the earth.

At some point, Evelyn had fallen asleep in the crook of his arm. He didn't move a muscle as she lay there, sleeping soundly under the blankets they had brought out throughout the night. He watched as her chest moved up and down, her body resting against his, her head nestled just under his chin.

He had a girlfriend.

He stifled a laugh and checked to see if he'd woken her. When her soft breathing continued, he returned his gaze to the sunrise, listening as bird songs rang out, praying this moment wouldn't end. He wanted to pinch himself. Could this really be happening? Evelyn was back in his arms after all this time?

Her phone dinged and she stirred. Then she jolted up, and when she saw him, she smiled.

"Good morning," he said.

"Good morning." She settled back into him. "I slept?"

He stretched his arms and legs, only to readjust them so she could get closer. "Like a baby."

She placed her hand on his chest. "It felt good."

They didn't move from their spot, watching the golden sunrise over the Atlantic Ocean. Boats dotted the horizon. Seagulls dipped into the waters as the waves curled onto the smooth sand shore. The sounds traveled perfectly through the hills like a natural amplifier. It was as if they were standing with their feet in the water.

He was afraid to move. To ruin the moment, or worse, end the moment. Things were so good. Too good. He couldn't help but worry because things never stayed good for Charlie. Things got muddled and mixed up and messy.

What would happen at the end of summer? Would Evelyn leave again? Would she stay year-round? If she left, where did that leave him? Would he be included in her plans?

He wanted to know, but he also didn't want to know. If he knew, he'd have to plan. He would calculate times, and it would create deadlines. He'd count down the days to an end, dreading the passing of another.

"I have to leave soon for my walk with the girls," she said, his fears coming true.

"Tell me I'll see you before tonight?" he asked.

"Would you like to stay?" she asked. "I can come back with breakfast."

He wanted so badly to say yes, but he had been gone too long. Harper would worry if she came over and he wasn't home, which he had a feeling she'd of course choose that morning to come over.

"I should head home and check in," he said.

"You're coming for dinner tonight still?" she asked.

He wrapped his arms around her, tightening his embrace. "Of course. Can't wait."

Her phone dinged again, but she didn't move like he feared. Instead, she leaned over and kissed him—a small kiss like they had been doing all night. God, he wanted this to last.

But like all things, the moment came to an end when a third ding hit her phone and she got up. He moved from his spot, suddenly stiff and sore and feeling his age. He rubbed his neck and moved all his limbs, making sure not to pull anything by doing so.

He stood and stretched as she walked into the house, rubbing his face with both hands. When was the last time he'd stayed up all night? He took in the view and leaned against the railing. The sun had already climbed high in the sky. Off in the distance, he spotted sanderlings scatter as a wave rolled into shore. Two kayakers floated across the horizon. From Evelyn's deck, he could see all of Gray Head and Sugar Beach. She had shown him her bedroom view. If she got permission to add on like she hoped, she'd have one of the best views on the island.

He peeked inside, checking on her, and saw her talking on the phone through the sliding glass doors. The old Buckley place hadn't seen better days in a real long time. Evelyn had quite the project on her hands. From what she told him, she wasn't going to hold back.

Pride rippled in his chest. He had been glad Evelyn wanted to help Harper, not only for the help but also for Harper to have a woman to look up to. Evelyn radiated confidence, was beautiful inside and out, and pursued a dream while continuing to learn and grow and strive to do better for herself. If there was one woman he could choose for his daughter to have as a mentor, it would be Evelyn.

When she finished her phone call, she returned with a coffee. "I'm sorry I'm taking off."

"While you enjoy your walk with your friends, I will enjoy this cup of coffee." He took the mug from her and grabbed hold of her hand. "Stop by the bookstore if you get a chance."

She smiled, which made her deep blues sparkle. A current of

longing rushed through him, and he took her into his arms and went to kiss her when a voice called out.

"Mom?" It was a woman's voice. A young woman's voice.

They both turned toward the voice, and that's when Charlie saw a younger version of Evelyn.

"Renee!" Evelyn broke out of Charlie's embrace and ran toward who he assumed was her daughter.

"Who is that?" her daughter asked, pointing to Charlie, not embracing Evelyn's hug. In fact, she stepped back, her face twisted. "Were you two about to kiss?"

Evelyn started laughing, a high-pitched laugh that sounded fake, and it made him cringe.

"What are you doing here?" Evelyn changed the subject.

Charlie looked around at the scene. Blankets thrown on the lounge chair, empty bottles of wine, two used glasses. He didn't know if he should explain or get out of there. He didn't want Evelyn's daughter to find out about him this way, but he noticed Evelyn hadn't acknowledged him.

"You didn't answer my question," her daughter snapped back.

That's when he took her cue. This was family business. Evelyn didn't want to talk in front of Charlie. Although, he thought the same thing as her daughter. Why didn't she answer the question? Was she thrown off by her daughter showing up? Was she embarrassed he was there?

"Renee, meet my good friend, Charlie." Evelyn held out her arm to him, as if she were announcing a contestant on a game show.

"Renee, it's really nice to meet you." He extended his hand to her.

Evelyn's daughter gave him a look as she crossed her arms over her chest. "Who are you?"

"Renee Irene," Evelyn scolded. "That is not how you greet a friend of mine."

Renee's eyes blazed with fire, and Charlie wished he had taken that cue.

"I should go." He put the mug on the table and was about to leave, when Evelyn put her hand on his arm.

"No, please. Renee must be tired from traveling." She narrowed her eyes at the young woman. "Please stay, enjoy your coffee. I should cancel my walk anyway." She turned away from Renee, placing her hand on his chest. "Please, stay."

He appreciated her standing up for him, but it wasn't fair on his part to be thinking of his feelings. Evelyn deserved to be able to have a conversation with her daughter about things. He didn't really blame Renee for being upset. She probably wasn't expecting her mom to be kissing some stranger.

"I bet you two need to catch up, and I need to get to the store." He rubbed her shoulder gently, hoping the anxiety that was all over her face would lessen once he left. "I'll see you later."

"Yes, dinner," she said. She kissed him on the cheek and turned toward Renee. "Let me help you with your things."

The two went inside the house, and that was that.

Charlie got into his truck and rubbed his eyes, exhaustion hitting him. He hoped and prayed Harper wasn't at the house, but when he got home, there she was, sitting in the kitchen with her own coffee, watching something on her phone.

"Stan!" she called out. "He's alive!"

Stan lifted his head off the couch, his tail wagging, and then laid back down.

"Thanks, Harp."

"You want to tell me why I had to leave my apartment last night to let out my father's dog?"

He could see her trying to hold back a smile. She was enjoying this.

"I appreciate you doing me a favor." He walked to the coffeepot and poured himself a large mug with a top. "I'm going to grab a shower."

"Are you seriously not going to tell me where you were last night?"

"I saw you and Mateo drive by, so I assume you know." He sipped his coffee, walking past her as her mouth dropped open.

"I was worried you might have been kidnapped!"

"You're a snoop."

"So . . .?" She followed him toward his room.

"You coming in the bathroom with me?" he asked, walking into the tiny space and holding the door open.

"No, but I can hear perfectly well through the door for all the details."

He shut the door. "Thanks again, Harper."

"Dad, come on. You have to tell me," she pleaded through the door.

He turned on the shower. "Goodbye, Harper!"

For good measure, he began to sing a little melody by Billy Joel and then moved on to Neil Diamond's "Sweet Caroline" over Harper's continuous questions. He hummed out his favorite jazz melody.

"Ugh!" she yelled through the door. "You are so impossible!"

He didn't need to play up his joyful mood. He would've sung that morning whether he was avoiding her or not. He was that happy. Even Renee didn't dampen his spirits. He was in love, and nothing would change that. Nothing.

Not until he left for the bookstore, did Harper give up. She stood at the door of the apartment when he left and said, "You're literally not going to tell me anything?"

"Literally."

He went to the bookstore to do some of the things he had been putting off but ended up on his computer. He gave kids who were dating these days credit. With social media and all the information someone could research, it was hard not to fall into a rabbit hole. Evelyn Rose had lots of information on the internet. By lunch, he felt like a stalker and incompetent.

"She's published seventy-something books," he said to Stan on their walk. "I've got two, and one was a flop."

He didn't walk the beach like usual. Instead, he walked downtown among the crowds of tourists piling on and off the ferry. Summer brought good things, like a cash flow that allowed him to relax a bit, but it also brought swamps of people who wanted a piece of the island to take home with them.

"Do you sell ornaments?" a woman asked as he and Stan walked back into the store.

"No, I'm sorry, we don't," he said. "There's a Christmas store on the corner of Harbor Lane and Main."

"Thank you!" the woman said and took off.

He turned to the person behind her and saw Evelyn.

"Evelyn!" He couldn't contain his delight. "It's nice to see you."

"Hi, Charlie." She smiled, but she bit her bottom lip, and his stomach became uneasy.

"What's up?" Now concerned, he stepped away from the counter. "You okay?"

"I feel terrible about how Renee treated you this morning." Her forehead scrunched in worry. "I'm so sorry."

"I have a daughter, I get it." Although he was sure Harper wouldn't have acted that way.

She smiled again, but he could tell it was forced. "Would you mind terribly if I postponed our dinner tonight?"

His stomach dropped like a mudslide, a heavy drag. He wiped his palms on the back of his pants. "Of course not."

He wanted to dig, to press. He wanted further explanation. But he didn't want to be that stupid young man he'd been before. The kid who allowed jealousy and insecurities to get in the way.

"Are you sure?" She bit her bottom lip again. "I just feel terrible."

"No need." He shook his head, playing cool. "You don't have to feel terrible."

There's no point having them both upset.

"Thank you for understanding," she said. "It's just, with Renee here, I want to have dinner with her."

"I totally understand." He walked around the counter and

stepped up to her. He cupped her elbows with both hands, drawing her close, intimate. "Let's have dinner another time."

Though he wanted to set a time and day right then, he hesitated. He'd wait for her to suggest it; he didn't want to come off needy. After all his research, he became very clear about one thing, Evelyn was not the same woman he had asked to marry him all those years ago.

The woman standing in front of him was a different person.

"Let's make it tomorrow."

He smiled. "That sounds perfect."

CHAPTER 22

"*A*re you like . . . dating this guy?" Renee asked in the kitchen as soon as she returned from seeing Charlie.

"You could say that." Evelyn couldn't believe her daughter's behavior. She hadn't been that embarrassed since she had to leave her grocery cart with the manager of Cub Foods and take her out, kicking and screaming. But Renee wasn't five, and Evelyn wasn't going to allow her daughter to treat someone she cared about like that.

"I want you to apologize when you see him next." Her knuckles hit her hip. Her mother stance. This wasn't a choice; it was a request.

"Who is he?" Renee didn't seem to notice.

"His name is Charlie Moran, and he's an old friend I've known for over thirty years." Evelyn laid it on thick.

"Thirty years?" This surprised Renee and why wouldn't it? Evelyn never once mentioned him. She'd talk about dating and had mentioned plenty about living on the island, but never once had she muttered Charlie's name to her daughters. She never allowed her daughters to know Evelyn Flannery.

And that made her sad.

She thought about Charlie and Harper's relationship. How

close they were. How they depended on each other for all the different areas in their life. She wanted that. And that meant she needed to be open and honest. She hadn't lied to her daughters, but she hid who she had been.

"I dated Charlie before I met your father." She needed to tell Renee. "He and I were engaged."

"You were engaged before Daddy?" Her jaw dropped. "Did Daddy know about him?"

She almost confessed about the cardinal that day on the lawn. Would Renee think she was a lunatic?

"Yes, your father knew all about Charlie." Evelyn reached out to brush Renee's hair away from her face. "I loved your father so much." But now, more than ever, she believed George had led her to this exact moment. She was almost certain. "Nothing will change that."

Renee played with her sleeve as Evelyn caught a tear about to fall off her chin. "Are you moving on?"

Evelyn didn't want to break her daughter's heart, but she had to speak her truth. "I will always love your father, but I'm ready to move on, yes."

Renee's eyes diverted, and she stepped back. She turned her back on Evelyn.

"What's going on, Renee?" Renee had been Daddy's little girl since the moment she was placed into his hands. She had followed him around the house all the way up to eighteen.

Renee hiccupped as she tried to catch her breath. She looked as though she was about to say something but walked out of the kitchen and onto the deck, shutting the screen door shut behind her.

Evelyn held the back of the chair and squeezed it, deciding to give her daughter a moment. As a little girl, Renee always needed to take time to herself before she calmed down. She'd run to her room and slam the door. George had taken it off its hinges when she was a teenager.

Evelyn took in a breath to regain her composure and stepped

out on the deck. "What made you change your mind to come to the island?"

"What?" Renee said, wiping her eyes with her shirt's sleeve.

"You told me you had too much work," Evelyn said. She was almost certain something else bothered Renee.

Renee crossed her arms, facing the water. The wind blew back her fine blond hair. Evelyn had loved to brush it out and style it. Renee, on the other hand, wanted nothing to do with French braids or double pigtails. She wanted blue jeans and dirt. Evelyn smiled thinking about the old birch tree Renee'd climb in their yard.

"I decided I needed a vacation." Renee shrugged, but tears continued to fall along her chin and dropped onto the deck boards.

Evelyn walked over to her daughter. "I'm sorry you found out this way."

"It's fine." Renee sniffled and wiped her eyes with her sweater's sleeve.

"Is there something else going on?" Her daughter's unexpected arrival seemed very unexpected. "When did you get to the island?"

"I left last night." Renee shook her head but didn't speak. "I just needed to leave. That's all. I just needed to get away."

Renee collapsed into Evelyn's arms and cried. She didn't tell her the rest of the story, and Evelyn didn't push. She just held Renee in her arms, rocking her back and forth like she had when she was a girl.

Renee had been her stoic daughter when George had passed away. It was as if she had read a manual on the proper etiquette for when someone died. She came home from Chicago right away. She helped with the arrangements, ran errands, made decisions when Evelyn couldn't keep herself together. She had been enduring, strong, and Evelyn had depended on her more than she realized until now. Her daughter was hurting.

"Why don't you get some rest," Evelyn suggested. "You can stay at my suite and just relax."

"Am I in the way?" Renee snapped at her.

"God no!" Evelyn shook her head. "I'm thrilled you're here. But there's going to be contractors here in a bit, and I have a gorgeous empty suite at the hotel."

Renee shook her head. "Do you mind if I just sit out on the deck and hang out with you?"

"Of course not." Evelyn tucked a loose strand of hair behind Renee's ear. She still had that little girl in there after all.

"Knock! Knock!" a voice called out.

"Who's that?" Renee asked.

"My assistant." Evelyn looked through the sliding doors, and walking in from the front door was Harper.

Harper called out again. She was dressed in a flowing bohemian floral dress with her hair tied up with a silk scarf. "I've got bagels."

She stopped when she saw Renee. "Hi."

"You have an assistant?" Renee asked.

Evelyn could see her daughter's shock. So much had happened. "Harper, meet my daughter Renee."

"Hi." Harper's face exploded in excitement. "Oh my God. I love your mother. It's so nice to meet you." She handed the container of bagels into Renee's hands. "I got them with lox and cream cheese."

Renee held the container but looked at Evelyn. "What else don't I know about your life?"

Evelyn's heart dropped. "Renee, it all just happened." She tilted her head. She understood Renee would be upset, but she never meant to hurt her. "It was never my intention to leave you out. I tried calling."

"Back to that again?' Renee looked at her as though Evelyn were a stranger.

"Come on, Renee." Evelyn dropped her hands by her side, surrendering.

"Thanks for the bagels," Renee said to Harper, but she dropped them on the picnic table and walked inside.

Evelyn couldn't believe what was happening. She listened as she heard the slam of a bedroom door from upstairs.

"Did I do something wrong?" Harper asked.

"No, you did nothing wrong." Evelyn made a face in apology. "I'm sorry. She's tired."

That's when she remembered about canceling dinner. "Harper, do you mind if I postpone dinner tonight?"

Harper shook her head. "Of course I don't mind."

When she talked to Charlie at the bookstore and told him she had to cancel dinner, he had been understanding, but she worried that he was just playing cool, and doubt crept into her mind. Maybe things were too good to be true. Maybe reality just hadn't caught up. Whatever brought Renee to the island, it was more than just a needed vacation. Something else was going on with Renee, and she was going to find out.

Evelyn had gone for a walk while Renee hid herself up in the room. When she returned, Renee stood in the kitchen with Wanda and Bitty and said to her, "You have roommates?"

Renee's eyes filled with moisture.

Evelyn's shoulders sagged, and she dropped her hands on the counter. She couldn't win with Renee.

"We got your text," Bitty said, while grimacing. "So we came to see if everything was okay, and I sort of let the cat out of the bag."

"When were you going to tell me about your new life?" Renee asked, and she sounded young, unsure.

"I wanted to tell you the other day when I called, but you let me go." Evelyn hadn't seen Renee this emotional in a long time.

"We should go," Wanda said.

"No, I think *I* should go." Renee took off down the wooden plank path down to the beach.

"Oh, sugar," Bitty said, rubbing Evelyn's arm. "I'm real sorry. I assumed she knew."

"It's not your fault." Evelyn sighed, watching as Renee started to run down the beach. "You ladies mind if I go and talk to her?"

"If she's upset about us staying, we certainly don't have to," Wanda said.

"This isn't about that," Evelyn reassured her. "I don't know what it's about, but I know it's not about you ladies. Let me go talk to her. But, please, go inside and stay. Look the place over, and think about what we need."

"Let us know if there's anything we can do," Bitty said.

"I will." Evelyn took in a deep breath and headed out toward the water. Memories of last night made her smile, even as she got more anxious about Renee.

"Want to tell me what's going on?" Evelyn cut right to the chase as she sat down in the sand next to Renee.

"Besides the fact you have a whole new life that I have no idea about?" Renee put her knees up to her chin and wrapped her arms around her legs, hugging them.

"Renee, I've been so empty." Evelyn had never told her daughters how she felt about anything. "When I lost Daddy, I felt as though I had no one."

"Gee, thanks," Renee said.

"You and Samantha had your own lives and had already moved out," she reminded her. "Besides, it's not fair of me to ask my children to stay around for me. I want you to be happy, but I want to be happy too."

"So you bought a house on an island?" Renee sounded as though this was insane.

"Yes." Evelyn wasn't going to make this a big deal anymore. Her daughter had the right to be upset about her surprise, but the moment was done. It was time to move on. "You should stay here."

"It looks like you're full." That's when Evelyn saw the pain, the hurt, the fear.

"Renee, wherever I am, I always want you and your sister to be able to come home."

"Who are those ladies?" she asked.

"They're my new friends." Evelyn peeked back to the house, watching as the two women she hardly knew walked along the deck. They had become some of the most important people in her life. "It's weird, but we all kind of found each other."

"And you're dating?" Renee's voice softened, and Evelyn knew this was more about George.

"Yes." Evelyn waited for her reaction.

"Were you going to tell us about him?" Renee asked.

Evelyn hadn't thought about telling the girls, because it had all just happened. "I honestly don't know what's going on, but I would have."

Evelyn placed her arm around her daughter's shoulders, holding her close to her side.

"Do you remember how shy you used to be when you were little?" Evelyn asked.

"Yes."

"We called you the clinger-oner." Evelyn laughed thinking about George at parties. It took interpersonal skills to be a doctor, or at least, it made George a wonderful doctor because of it. He could talk to anyone. "But secretly, I was the clinger-oner. I clung to your father. I clung to you girls. I clung to the house."

She could feel the familiar weight piling on her shoulders, pulling her down.

"I'm not trying to be a jerk," Renee said. "It's just hard to think of you with another man. I miss him so much."

"I miss him too." Evelyn tensed her jaw to pull back the emotion. She needed to be strong for Renee. "Let it out, Renee. You need to let it all out."

Renee began to sob, deep, wrenching cries that shook her whole body. Evelyn didn't know how she kept it together, but she sat next to Renee, rubbing her back, telling her she would be okay. The waves covered her sounds, but she continued to rub her back long after her sobs quieted down, and her breath steadied.

When Evelyn brushed Renee's hair away from her face, she could tell something else was going on with her daughter, but she wouldn't push it.

The familiar tightness around her chest didn't cease once Renee stopped crying, or when they went back to the house and met the girls. Or even when Renee relaxed and talked about Chicago and laughed at Bitty's story of working in the Windy City.

"I'd stood outside Harpo Studios to try to be in the audience of *Oprah* so many times!"

By the afternoon, Renee asked the ladies to join them for dinner, and by dinner, Renee whispered to Evelyn, "I can see why you like them so much."

But the tightening didn't stop, the anxiety prickling up Evelyn's legs and chest didn't slow down. The panic of things falling apart overwhelmed her rational thoughts. Nothing was going to happen. She wasn't going to lose anything. Or anyone. *Things will be okay*, she kept repeating in her head, but as they sat down for dinner, Evelyn wondered what she was going to do if she lost them too.

CHAPTER 23

That night, Renee stayed at the house with Evelyn for the first time. They made up the bedrooms, including Evelyn's king-sized bed on the third floor that sat in the middle of the room to face the water. She wanted to wake up looking at the ocean.

They called Samantha together by video, and Evelyn let Renee tell the news and show off the house.

"I can't believe you bought a beach house," Samantha said, and unlike her sister's reaction, she sounded thrilled.

"It's adorable," Renee said, now sounding excited about it all. Evelyn knew it would be only a matter of time. Everyone fell in love with the Vineyard. "You have to come back to the states and see it."

Evelyn smiled to herself as Renee continued showing the rest of the house. Then, like a wave building up as it came to shore, the shortness of breath returned, and her anxiety continued to crawl up her neck.

What was she doing? Could she live on this island? Was she being irresponsible with her money? Should she have talked to a financial advisor? Should she have had a second inspection? Should she blow this kind of money on a century-old beach house? Was she being selfish and making Renee go along with it?

"Where on the island?" Samantha asked as Renee came back into the living room.

"Eastport, along the Vineyard Sound," Evelyn said, her throat suddenly dry.

"I want to come," Samantha whined.

"Come." Evelyn didn't hesitate. She could even give the girls the third floor to give them more privacy.

"I caught mom kissing a man," Renee said.

"Renee!" Evelyn couldn't believe her. She hadn't expected her to tell.

"Mom was kissing a man?" Samantha screeched. Evelyn braced herself for her youngest to have a similar reaction, but instead she said, "Alright, Mom!"

Evelyn looked at Samantha on Renee's screen.

"Is he handsome?" she asked.

Renee shrugged. "Not as handsome as Daddy, but handsome like George Clooney."

Evelyn could feel her cheeks flush at the image.

"Oh!" Samantha shook her eyebrows up and down. "Mom has a special someone."

She started to say something, to deny it, but stopped. "Yes, he is special."

Renee dropped the phone to her side and stared at her. "You two are that serious? It's been a week."

Evelyn didn't want another morning event, yet she wasn't going to deny anymore or hide the truth, which was that she wanted, no needed, to move on.

"I think I'm falling for him," she said.

Renee's mouth dropped wide open.

"Hello?" Samantha called from the phone. "I'm still here. I can't hear."

The two women stood facing each other, but Evelyn wasn't going to bend, not even as her anxiety pulsated throughout her body. She couldn't second-guess her decisions now, not even if that upset Renee. She had just begun feeling life again—good again.

And she wasn't going to let that go. Even if it had been a week, she wanted another and another and another after that. She wanted to finish this house and care for her friend and kiss Charlie. And she wasn't going to feel bad about it. She didn't want to hurt her daughter but wanted to live life again.

"Yes, even after just a week."

Renee's shoulders drooped, but she didn't say anything more about it, even after Samantha asked about twenty questions. She didn't tell her sister about how Evelyn had been engaged to this man or how she had roommates. Renee didn't talk at all until she hung up with Samantha.

"I'm sorry that this is all difficult for you," Evelyn said.

But Renee shook her head and said, "I'm pregnant."

Evelyn's heart exploded with joy, but Renee fell onto the couch, her head in her hands, her shoulders shaking. Renee was crying.

Evelyn froze, stunned by her daughter's reaction. Evelyn sat slowly down next to Renee, leaning next to her and squeezing her in her arms.

"I'm going to be a Grammy?" she squealed in a whisper, kissing Renee's head. "What wonderful news."

Everything made much more sense.

"When did you find out?"

"A few days ago," Renee said. "I had hoped . . ."

She cried harder, and she couldn't get the words out.

"Shush," Evelyn whispered. "This is wonderful news."

She decided not to ask any questions, to let Renee tell her why she was so upset. But she wondered where Harry fit in at this point. His absence was suddenly very glaring.

"I just left," Renee said. "I didn't even tell him I was leaving. I just walked out." Renee's chest heaved up and down.

"Does Harry know about the baby?" Evelyn didn't understand.

Why did Renee leave her husband? She had thought her daughter was happy.

"He wants nothing to do with me or the baby."

Evelyn stiffened as a strong wave of protectiveness took over her body. "I will take care of you and the baby."

"I couldn't stay in Chicago, in that restaurant when he wants nothing to do with us." She sobbed. "I had to leave."

"You can stay here as long as you need," Evelyn said, rubbing her daughter's back, trying to sound reassuring even though she wasn't sure what they were going to do. Pregnant? Her baby was pregnant? And Harry left her? "We will make this work."

"You already have the women staying here," she said.

"And there's plenty of room for my daughter and grandbaby. Look, you are my daughter, and I will help you and your baby no matter what." Evelyn brushed Renee's hair with her hand. "I love this baby already."

"I do too," Renee said through hiccups. "I just thought he'd step up, but he . . ." She started to cry harder and leaned into Evelyn. Was this what Evelyn had felt coming? The worry that haunted her all day?

But the news only made her squeeze her daughter closer. As the anxiety tingled up her arms and chest, she said, "This is wonderful news. I can't wait to be a Grammy."

"Are you sure you don't mind me staying?" Renee asked.

"You're always welcome," she said.

But she worried about the ladies and her promises to them. Would this upset them? Would they not want to stay on? Would Wanda leave and be by herself with cancer?

"I promised the women they could stay on as well," she said to Renee. "I hope you can understand if they do."

This wasn't a question. She would keep her promises.

Renee nodded, taking in a shaking breath. "I can help around here. I can even pay rent and stuff."

Evelyn rubbed her back. "The first thing we should do is get you to a doctor and see how everything is progressing."

Renee wiped her eyes with the back of her hands and looked up at Evelyn. "I love you, Mom. I'm sorry I freaked out."

"I love you too." Evelyn tilted her head, her eyebrows pressing together in concern. "You were upset, and we're all allowed to react badly sometimes."

She put Renee to bed under the new duvet cover in the king-sized bed. She'd give Renee the top floor. She could make it into an in-law suite with its own private bath and kitchenette for her and the baby.

By morning, Renee seemed calm. Her eyes were still puffy, but when Evelyn pulled up a website for baby furniture, she started to sound excited about becoming a mother.

"Nana was a single mom," Renee said about George's mother.

Evelyn had forgotten about that. "Yes, she raised a fine son."

Evelyn handed her daughter a mug of warm lemon water instead of coffee and they sat out on the deck.

"Are you sure I'm not in the way of your new life here?" Renee asked, looking out at the water.

"Only enhancing it," she said, shaking her head. "I love the idea of you and the baby moving here with me."

She'd know George would insist it if he were alive. He had always said he'd split up their one-acre lot for the girls to be able to build their own homes if they'd want. She joked about making children move on but also liked the idea of them that close.

"What about the house in Minnesota?" Evelyn had thought about offering the house, but hesitated. "I'm not sure if I'm going back."

Renee only nodded, but she hoped her daughter understood. If she went back to Minnesota, she'd be setting herself back in a place where she could no longer breathe. No longer live. No longer move on or let go. She couldn't go back to the house; she didn't even want to go back to visit at this point. Too many memories. Too many dark memories. She wanted to give time, along with space, to let them fade and allow the good memories, the ones she kept dear to her heart, to float above.

"I want to stay here for now," Renee said. "At least until the baby comes."

For the first time since her daughter's arrival, Evelyn felt a sigh of relief. She didn't know what her plans were for the house back home, but as far as she was concerned, she could take time to think about what was best for the three of them.

"I missed you a lot," Evelyn confessed, wrapping her arms around her daughter like she had when she was little.

"I missed you too."

That afternoon, when Renee took a nap, Evelyn went into town to meet the ladies at the hotel.

"So that's the situation." She had laid out everything that happened.

Bitty and Wanda looked at each other across the coffee table in the suite.

Bitty crossed her hands on her lap and said, "Well, I just love babies."

Tears sprung into Evelyn's eyes, and she looked to Wanda. "Do you feel comfortable going through all this with a baby?"

Wanda sat still, calm, staying silent longer than Evelyn could barely take, but then she said, "I think that it would be an honor to be a part of all of this."

"Three old ladies and a baby," Bitty said, and the ladies started laughing together at the joke.

Evelyn's chest loosened a bit, and she took in a deep breath, glad that having her daughter stay didn't change their minds and grateful to have met such amazing women.

"Dinner tonight at the house," she said.

"We talked about pitching in with the renovations as a way to repay you for your kindness," Wanda said as Bitty nodded.

Evelyn shook out her arms. "No, absolutely not. This is my adventure, and I'm dragging you all along. This is all on me."

Bitty placed her hand on Evelyn's and said, "We want to be able to help in some way."

Evelyn looked at the both of them. "You have no idea how much you all have helped already."

All three women leaned into each other, taking each other's hands. A promise told through their embrace.

When she left The Wharf and walked down Harbor Lane toward the bookstore she stopped before crossing the street and stared at the bookstore.

She knew what needed to happen. The next step, the next way to loosen the grip of pain, to be able to feel again. She stepped onto the cobblestone road and walked up to the front door of the store, looking in the window. The bell rang against the glass as she opened the door, stepped inside, and looked at the front counter for him.

She didn't see him or Stan, but there was an older woman stacking books on a shelf.

"Excuse me," Evelyn said to the woman. "Is Charlie Moran here?"

The woman frowned. "No, I'm afraid you just missed him."

"Do you know where I might find him?" She wondered if she was being pushy.

But the woman didn't seem to think it strange that some random woman was asking where her boss was. "He usually takes his dog for walks along the beach at this time."

Ah, she remembered. He walked Stan along Sugar Beach.

As she walked out of the store, she put her purse strap over her shoulder and began to jog through the crowds of tourists to the beach. She took off her sandals and walked barefoot along the packed sand, looking for Charlie. She had never been more certain this was what she wanted. Charlie was what she wanted. She wanted to explore this new relationship. She wanted to be able to fall in love again. To kiss a man again. To kiss a man a lot again.

She wanted the fairy tale.

Just as she was about to get close to Sea View, she saw him walking. He stopped when he saw her. She waved her arm high so he could see her, but he didn't wave back. He just stood there.

"Charlie!" she called out as she jogged up to meet him and Stan. "I'm so glad I found you."

He didn't move as Stan wagged his tail and pulled on his leash to reach her.

She slowed as she noticed his expression appeared solemn, hard.

"Hey," she said, wrinkling her brow in concern.

"Hello, Evelyn," he said.

"I was hoping to find you," she said, suddenly feeling like she was an unwelcome intrusion and needed to explain herself. "I stopped at the store and they said you were on a walk."

He nodded but looked at the water.

"Are you okay?" she asked without thinking, but feeling a strange energy coming from him.

"No, I don't think I am," he said.

Her heart dropped. This was the moment she had dreaded. The moment her body had been preparing for.

"I'm sorry I canceled dinner," she said. "Renee isn't upset anymore."

He stuffed his hands into his pockets. "It's not that. It's just that I'm not ready to be part of something that can just be canceled on a whim."

Her heart dropped. "I am sorry I canceled, but my children come first."

"Of course, and I'm not asking you to change that," he said, but this only made her more confused.

"Come tonight. Meet Renee," she urged. "She is going through some stuff. She has totally calmed down."

"I am really glad you came to the island, and I am really happy for you with the house and you're writing again," he said. "But I think it's better if we do the neighbor thing rather than anything more for now."

"What?" She couldn't believe what was happening. "Why?

What happened?" She didn't understand. She had just canceled dinner. "I thought you understood?"

"I did. I do," he said. He didn't look her way.

"Well, it sure doesn't seem like it." She was a bit annoyed. Her daughter was upset. Did he really want her to have a dinner party that badly?

"Evelyn, I'm really sorry, but I just can't," he said, and this time, he looked her straight in the eyes. He was filled with pain and sadness. "I just can't."

He didn't move, just stood, waiting for her to make the next move, say the next thing. But when she didn't, he said, "Good luck, Evelyn. I hope everything works out for you and your family."

She didn't speak; she couldn't. She didn't know what to say. Her heart felt as though it were tearing, pulling from her ribcage, ripping out of her chest.

She watched as he gave her one last nod and left her standing there, alone.

CHAPTER 24

"*I*t's the best thing for her, believe me," he said as he got into his truck.

"I can't believe you just dumped her like that on the beach," Harper said, ripping mad. She was angrier than the time he'd told her she couldn't go to her junior prom with that kid from Boston. "She was devastated when she came back, and that set off the daughter, who, if you ask me, is already a little off."

Charlie didn't mean to set anyone off, but he knew it would only hurt a little now instead of truly devastating her in the end. A guy like him was no good for a woman as wonderful as Evelyn.

Dr. George Rose was the knight in shining armor, not a high school dropout who failed at his career, couldn't write, lived off his aunt's dole, and whose only friend was his daughter. No way. The other night had been magical, but like all magic, it wasn't real. Her daughter had walked in, reminded him he was no good for a woman like Evelyn. No good at all.

Look at how his life had ended up. He lived above a dumpy old bookstore with his dog. He didn't need to compare himself to the man who was actually saving lives, not just writing about them. And he didn't even write anymore.

He had been ridiculous to think he was good enough for a

woman like her. It would only be a matter of time until she figured it out herself. No, he didn't need to be left again like she left him in the past, or like when Tanya left him when his career fell apart, or when his dad left when being a husband and a father was too hard. No, it was better this way.

He started the engine and gave Harper a look. "I'm headed to the mainland. I'll be back in a couple of days."

"Dad, don't be this way. Go talk to her. You're being ridiculous," she said.

"Harper, I've asked you enough to stay out of this." His voice was hard. Harper stepped back.

"You can get all bent out of shape, but you know I'm right." Harper shook her head. "You're being super stupid stubborn!"

He wanted to argue, but instead, he said, "I love you, kid," rolled up his window and took off. He'd get on that ferry and get off this island.

He had plenty of time when he pulled his truck onto the ferry. He left his truck and ventured up on the top deck. The summer day had been perfect—sunny and bright; not a cloud in the sky, and with a soft breeze just enough to cool the heat. He took a seat next to the railing, looking out at the island, looking at the familiar landmarks that marked the passage of his life. The harbor where he fished with his dad before he'd skipped town. The tiny house he'd stayed in with his mother before she died. The bookstore that had saved his broken soul with the apartment he lived in with Harper.

It was obvious Evelyn came to the island for closure, and that's what he gave her. He allowed her to move on from the death of her husband like he allowed her to recover from the pain of being hurt by her first boyfriend that summer. Charlie wasn't the guy *for* her, but the one who helped her find her way. It would be only a matter of time before Evelyn finds another knight in shining armor. She deserved more than a failure like him.

She dropped millions on a whim. She stayed in the best suite on Martha's Vineyard. She didn't need a guy who couldn't retire even if he wanted to.

He brought nothing to the relationship, and Evelyn needed more than what he could give her. She had been so generous, so giving, so willing to share everything she had. She didn't need someone to leech off her goodwill and kindness. And he certainly didn't want to be the man she had to help.

He couldn't provide anything for her.

And that bothered him.

A lot.

He watched as the island disappeared, fading away in the horizon. Harper was right. He was stubborn and stupid, but that didn't change the fact Evelyn was way out of his league.

What now, Charlie? he thought to himself. He had no plans. He hadn't even tried to cover shifts and figure out a plan with the bookstore. He had just told Harper if they wanted to work, great; if not, keep the store closed. He didn't care at this point. When was the last time he took a vacation anyway?

When the ferry reached Falmouth Harbor, he jumped into his truck and took off for the city. He didn't know what he would do when he got there, but he needed the crazy of the city to drown out the crazy in his head. How could he have been so stupid falling for her again? How could he have even thought someone like her would be happy with someone like him? Only Harper had stayed in his life, and he was sure it was out of loyalty.

He pounded the steering wheel. He had everything he ever wanted within his grasp, and he'd screwed it up again.

He drove up route three all the way to the city to downtown. He parked close to Yawkey Way but immediately headed back toward the Boston Gardens. He walked along the streets with no real plan in mind other than going to see the Sox play and getting his mind out of the clouds. Before Evelyn had shown up, he'd been good. Life had been decent. He had a rhythm, and it worked for him. He had dated and had a friend from time to time, but he had Harper and the bookstore. He had his side things, and his friends. He didn't need to go chasing the past.

He walked through the public gardens to Beacon Street, then followed along side streets with no destination in mind. He didn't know what he was doing, but suddenly he stood outside a bookstore. It sat inside the familiar red brick buildings, its windows filled with new releases and popular titles, and right smack in the middle sat an Evelyn Rose.

He had been the antagonist in her series. The guy who broke the heroine's heart and scarred her trust. He had been the evil husband who damaged her, made her reluctant to love again. He was the bad guy.

He stepped inside the bookstore. The familiar smells of print filled the air around him.

"Can I help you?" a woman asked from behind a shelf.

He shook his head. "No, thank you. I'm good."

He didn't need help finding what he was looking for. He, better than most, knew how bookstores carried their titles. Popular titles were always front and center. It took three display tables to find more of her books. The popular television series now donned the books' covers. The actress stood on Gray Head at the edge of the cliffs, looking out at the sound.

He grabbed the first book, the one he remembered reading, the one where the heroine was saved by the handsome doctor on the island. He read the back cover, but it displayed her awards and award-winning author five-star reviews. He put the book back in its place on the display and picked up another title, *The Journal*. On the right corner of the cover, it read "Newest release!" He picked up the hardcover and opened to the blurb on the inside.

He froze after reading the first few sentences. Never in a million years would he forget the first story she'd worked on with him. She had spent all summer tweaking, planning, and prepping while he read and critiqued, helped her set the emotion, build the tension, and she'd shown him all the different techniques her professors taught her. He'd spin all their advice and suggest she break all their rules.

"Just because they do it that way doesn't mean it's right." He'd read different female authors like Virginia Woolf or Charlotte Brontë or Toni Morrison and show her their style. That book had been the beginning of everything.

He flipped to the end, where the acknowledgements were written, and there was his name.

I'd like to thank the first person that ever challenged me. Who strengthened my writing and pushed me further, harder, than anyone I've ever met. The person who taught me how to love writing and so much more. Charlie Moran.

He almost dropped the book.

He turned to the copyright. It had been printed the year before. She had been thinking about him a year before?

What the heck did this mean?

He had an urge to call Harper, tell her about the book. Did she know? Had she read this book yet?

He suspected she hadn't; otherwise, she definitely wouldn't have let him leave the island.

He picked up the book and brought it to the counter.

"Find everything you were looking for?" the woman asked.

He nodded. "Yes, thank you."

He paid and took the book without a receipt or a bag. The second he walked out onto the street, he looked for a bench and saw a T-station close by. As soon as he sat down, he opened to the first page, and read.

CHAPTER 25

*A*fter another week staying at The Wharf, Bitty and Wanda officially checked out and moved into Sea View.

Evelyn did everything she could to forget her talk with Charlie by busying herself getting ready for Bitty and Wanda to come to the house. She included Renee in all the decisions. First, they met with an interior designer who was located there on the island. Mateo drew up designs for the town. Mateo had a good feeling about being approved. Other projects had no trouble getting permits for similar work, which was encouraging.

Next, they shopped. A lot. They ferried to the mainland and took the train downtown. They started with Renee's bedroom combined nursery, which would be on the third floor for now. Evelyn had plans for the detached garage when the house was finished. By then, the baby would be older and Renee would feel more confident as a mother. There was a small space above, not big enough to live with a baby, but maybe the whole thing could be converted into a guest cottage, or maybe even rebuilt.

The week went by in a blur. She filled her days with errands and meetings and writing—lots and lots of writing. The novel she had started at the beginning of this adventure had poured out of her, but now she was stuck in the weeds. She needed to figure out how to properly end the book, but the fog Charlie promised to lift clung around her, not allowing the light to come through. So, she kept writing and writing and shopping and running around.

When Bitty and Wanda arrived at Sea View with their things, she and Renee met them at the front door, welcoming them inside. They helped carry their bags up to the bedrooms on the second floor. They brought Wanda to her room first, which Renee dubbed the East Room. The east wall had a view of the morning sunrise coming up over the cliffs of Gray Head. They painted the room a soft blue and found white linens. The room appeared bright and airy and bigger than its small space.

"I love it!" Wanda clapped her hand to her chest. "It's beautiful."

She walked to the hand-knit blanket Harper had found at a craft fair on the island.

"You did all this in a week?" Bitty exclaimed, walking around the room, stroking the duvet with her palm. "This is gorgeous."

Evelyn was pleased her friends liked it. "I want you and Wanda to feel absolutely at home."

She had purchased extras for their rooms like a cushy area rug for the wood floor, a soft leather recliner and ottoman for the corner of each room, along with a standing lamp beside it. The day she and Bitty went to the art gallery in town, she had picked out a few paintings, which she hung above the beds and along the walls. She had Mateo's workers put up drapes and ordered customized shelving for the closets.

A cleaning service came to the house and deep cleaned the whole place, which had been money well spent. The bathrooms and kitchen gleamed; the musty, moldy scents gone. Now there were only the smells of new construction and the briny scent of sea.

The week had brought pleasant surprises, like the friendship growing between Renee and Harper. At first, she wasn't sure if her daughter would open up to this stranger, but when Harper showed up on her Vespa, Renee became intrigued. Evelyn had no doubt the two would become fast friends.

"Have you read *My Life in France* by Julia Child?" Harper asked Renee.

"No," Renee said, as Harper set down her helmet on the table. "Should I?"

"Yes." Harper handed her a copy of the book. "I brought my copy with me."

"I can't take your book." Renee passed it back to Harper, but Harper ignored the book and started listing the titles. "Evelyn, you should stock the shelves with all your favorite books."

Evelyn smiled at the idea, but Charlie flashed through her mind, and her heart dropped again.

"Has Charlie returned from his trip?" Evelyn asked Harper, a bit embarrassed she had broken her silent promise. She didn't want to ask about Charlie. She didn't want to know he'd taken off and needed time away. She didn't want to think about the fact he hadn't texted or messaged or sent any type of communication since that day on the beach. It had been almost a whole week, and she had heard nothing from him.

Usually, she didn't have to ask. Harper didn't hold back on her feelings, and in the midst of decorating and errands and grocery shopping with Renee, Harper convinced her daughter that she and Charlie were destined for each other.

"He'll be back soon," Harper said confidently. "You guys are like lobsters."

Evelyn didn't know much about lobsters, but if he came back, would he talk to her again? Would they have any relationship after he got back? Or would they end everything and become strangers again?

The next surprise from the week was that Bitty ran into a local gynecologist she had worked with in Boston years ago.

"You'll love her. She's the best of the best," Bitty said to Renee, when she came with them to the first appointment.

The biggest surprise was how emotional she became when

they heard the baby's heartbeat. She melted the second she heard the strong little thumping coming from the machines.

"Do you want to find out the sex?" the doctor asked.

"Yes, please," Renee said, squeezing Evelyn's hands as the doctor moved the wand of the ultrasound around.

"Well, Mom, it looks like you will be having a little boy." The doctor pointed to the screen at a 3D image. Evelyn couldn't contain her tears as she looked at the most beautiful image of her grandson.

"I want to name him George," Renee said on the way back to the house.

Evelyn could hardly push down the lump in her throat to respond. "I think that's a perfect name for the first grandson."

Renee still hadn't discussed what happened between her and Harry and Evelyn didn't push it. She had offered to purchase plane tickets to go back to the city with Renee, thinking she'd feel comfortable going with her, but Renee turned the offer down. She wondered when, if ever, Renee would open up to her about everything.

That night, as Renee made the main dish for dinner, the ladies sat around the small island and helped with everything else.

"Let's eat on the deck," Evelyn suggested, grabbing some plates and dinnerware.

"Let me set the table," Harper said, pulling open the silverware drawer.

"Let me open a bottle of champagne to mark the occasion." Bitty pulled out a chilled bottle from the refrigerator and poured each of them a glass and a sparkling cider for Renee. She held up her glass as vegetables sizzled on the pan.

"To Sea View! May our friendships last as long as the ocean," Evelyn said aloud.

"To Sea View!" they all responded.

They clinked glasses together, but Wanda stopped Evelyn before taking a drink. "To Evelyn and Renee." Wanda wrapped her arm around Evelyn's waist and squeezed. "Thank you for opening your home to us."

Evelyn held her glass against her friends' and looked at each one of their faces. She knew she should be happy. She set out to find this, a community of friends, her daughter and her soon-to-be grandchild staying with her, a home filled with love and joy. She had been fulfilled in her career and now had a beautiful view she had always dreamed about. She didn't need anything more.

"Oh no!" Renee cried out, running outside onto the deck. A seagull dangled above the breadbasket, clawing at a roll.

Renee swung her arms at the bird, but it didn't fly away, even as Renee continued to shoo it from the table. It floated above, fluttering its wings, dipping down close and then settling on the railing.

"He's a pesky bugger, isn't he?" Bitty said, joining Renee out on the deck, waving her arms out at the bird.

As soon as Bitty got close, it lifted off the railing and landed right on the edge of the roof, just high enough where Bitty couldn't reach. "I guess he's staying for dinner."

Evelyn laughed.

"Okay, George," she said to herself.

"What's that?" Wanda asked.

She shook her head, smiling. "Nothing."

She pulled out her phone. It was time. She was ready. George may never have told what he would hope for her if he were to die, but she knew the answer.

He would want her to be happy.

She opened the screen and went to Charlie's number and typed, **Come back to the island.**

Then she took a photo of the cliffs reddening from the sunset's reflection, falling behind the clouds.

She placed her phone on the counter and carried a bowl of pasta and fresh salad out to the table on the deck. They bowed their heads as Bitty said grace.

Evelyn sat quiet throughout dinner, thinking, observing, and reflecting. She had a good life, one that many would be envious of. She was happy and in a much better place now than she had been months ago. She had a long way to go, but she had already set up a date with a new grief therapist, had plans to return to the house in a few months before Christmas, and had talked to a financial advisor.

Apparently, George had done a good job setting up their finances. Their 401ks, mutual funds, and stocks were all worth a lot—more than she had thought. Not to mention the life insurance pay out and trust funds George's grandfather had given him. He had made sure she and the kids would be taken care of in case the worst happened.

When they finished dinner and started cleaning up, it was Harper who gasped first, then Wanda. And Bitty said, "You old dog, you."

Evelyn didn't turn at what they all stared at, not sure what she'd see until she saw a flock of seagulls taking flight above the water.

Then she saw Charlie.

"You're back," she said, holding a stack of dishes in her hands.

"I'm in. I'm all in." He stood at the edge of the deck with Stan by his side. "And I want this. I want you. I want us. I don't know why I got spooked, but I was happy, and I just want to make you happy. And I think I could make you happy."

Evelyn didn't move; she just held the dishes in her hands. The other women froze, waiting for her to do something.

"Say something!" Renee said from the other side of the table.

"Put the dishes down and kiss the man," Wanda suggested.

Bitty leaned over and removed the plates from Evelyn's hands.

"But you left," Evelyn said. "You said you couldn't do this." She motioned her hands between them. "I don't need to be dragged around emotionally."

Charlie walked up to her and pulled out a familiar book.

"You found it," she whispered.

She had written it the summer they met. The first book she ever wrote from beginning to end. In her opinion, it would always be her best book. It had been like her first child—she had been so protective of it that she put it away for another day. But when Charlie left for California and they'd broken up, she never wanted to look at it again. She had put it in the bottom of a drawer until she'd needed something for her editor. She'd dug it out, revised it, and edited it through a new lens. She had seen things clearer, more focused. She'd been less naïve and more knowledgeable about life and its circumstances, and she revised the ending.

"You gave us a happily ever after." He held up the book. "You believed in us all this time?"

She shook her head. "No. I don't know. I was a fool to think we could make it work."

"Did you just come here to heal old wounds?" His eyes were intense. "Or did you come here because you still feel something for me?"

She closed her eyes as she took in a deep breath. There were few moments in her life that changed the course of it, and fewer that she recognized in real time, but she knew the next moment would forever alter what came next. She wanted to slow time down, feel the sea breeze blowing against her face. Feel the last bit of heat from the evening sunlight against her skin. Taste the sea salt in the humid air.

"I came to the island because that feeling never went away," she admitted. "I loved my husband, and I always will, but I never got over you."

Charlie wrapped his arms around her waist, swinging her into his embrace, and whispered to her, "I've never stopped loving you, Evelyn, and I never will."

And with that, he leaned her over, dipping her into his hold, sweeping her into his arms, and he kissed her.

Behind them, the women erupted in cheers and clapping. Wanda awed as Bitty gave a whistle. Harper shook Renee and pointed at them, laughing and saying, "See, I told you they were lobsters."

When Charlie finally brought Evelyn back to her feet, she whispered, "Where have you been?"

"I've been writing." He held her close to him, smiling at her.

She kissed him again, wrapping her arms around his neck, letting the girls cheer even louder. She didn't care; she wouldn't stop. Evelyn had found her happily ever after.

CHAPTER 26

*A*fter a month living at Sea View, Evelyn had a whole new routine. She no longer woke at three thirty, but instead, woke to the sun. Sometimes, she got up before it rose, waiting for it to peek above the horizon line, its rays filtering through the clouds as she watched the kaleidoscope of colors. Other times, she'd let its warmth kiss her face, gently lulling her awake. She lived for those sunrises. The moment when life's miracles showed off the most.

It was at that time she'd talk to the seagulls, or the sparrows, or the sanderlings scurrying along beyond the tidal pools and seagrass. She'd fill George in on all the goings on—all the new appointments Renee had, how big Baby George was getting inside Renee's belly.

"She's even calling him G for short." She laughed at how Renee talked to him, calling the baby G. *"Hey, G, stop kicking me."*

She took a sip of coffee, another wonderful change in the routine. Chef Renee Rose lived with her, not the angsty teenager who had dirty laundry lying around, but a five-star chef who made an amazing espresso or latte or regular cup of coffee, along with souffles and buttery croissants and seafood entrées only found in Michelin-star restaurants. Renee cooked for every meal and most of the appetizers for game nights on Tuesday, which included Hank and Anita from the writers' group, and Phil and his partner Andre. She packed healthy lunches for when the girls traveled to the city for Wanda's treatments on Tuesdays so they wouldn't have to eat at the hospital's cafeteria. And last night, she even provided cookies and treats for after their writers' group.

"The girls and I haven't missed a day of walking, and I've lost some weight," she announced to George, feeling encouraged. She still had an extra ten pounds she'd like to shed, but with Renee's desserts, she wasn't sure how she would. "Although Renee keeps making these amazing meals with at least a stick of butter."

She thought about the five cookies she ate last night at the writers' group. She had been so nervous. She had finished her final draft of her latest book, a story of a woman overcoming the loss of her husband. She finally figured out her happy ending. All she had to do in the end was just write it.

"I had it in me all along," she said, letting out a laugh at herself. Funny how life worked.

Usually, once she finished her little chat with George, she and the girls walked if the weather permitted. Both Wanda and Bitty usually woke up after her, and they'd all head out. Sometimes Renee would join them, but the three women tried never to miss a day.

Wanda insisted they walk every day, even through her chemotherapy treatments.

"The salty air is good for me," she'd say.

The salty air helped Evelyn too. It loosened her mind and allowed her to think about what she planned on writing for the day. They would walk to the cliffs and back, about two full miles, and retreat to their spaces when they returned.

Then Evelyn would write. She wrote mostly outside, under the umbrella in her lounge chair. She even bought one of those visors Wanda always raved about. She used the sun as her pace, the waves as her pulse, and the wind as her guide.

This morning, though, Evelyn skipped writing. Instead,

Charlie had made plans. Secret plans he even kept from Harper and Renee.

Wanda stepped out onto the deck. An early riser like Evelyn and Renee, she looked worn, yet she always showered and dressed as if she were attending a fancy event.

"You should be resting," Evelyn said, her concern coming out in her voice.

"I feel okay this morning," Wanda said. "I'm tired, but okay."

Evelyn pushed the cream toward Wanda as she sat.

"Is today the big day?" Wanda asked.

Evelyn wondered how big this day really was. He had told her to pack a bag. She had never been on a romantic adventure where she had no idea where she was going. She had so many questions, which Charlie would patiently answer.

"Do I need a cocktail dress? Is it formal? Or should I just bring outdoorsy clothing? Will we be near water?"

"Yes, yes, and yes." He gently kissed her on the lips. "And bring sunscreen."

She packed everything. A new black strapless dress she'd picked up at Nordstrom's when they were in the city for Wanda's treatment. A one-piece swimsuit that made those extra ten pounds part of her curves, not just a big butt. Running shoes along with running gear. She started a new goal with Charlie.

"Am I making too big of a deal?" She looked at the large piece of luggage in the kitchen. She slapped her forehead. "He's going to think I'm insane."

"Has he watched *Real Housewives*?" Renee asked. "Two pieces of luggage for a weekend away is a very acceptable amount."

Oh God, she hoped she hadn't overtalked this whole surprise-date thing.

"He's just taking me up north, that's all."

Wanda smiled. "I really like that Charlie."

Evelyn cupped her mug and thought about Charlie's easy-going nature, his charismatic personality once he opened up, and his mind—oh, that mind of his. The way he thought so deeply and passionately about everything made her swoon. Not to mention how time had only made him more handsome.

The sliding door opened, and Bitty stepped out in her golf attire.

"Do you have ladies' putters this morning?" Wanda asked, now sipping a glass of orange juice.

"Sure do." Bitty curtsied and twirled around in her new outfit. "I've got my own lunch affair afterward."

"With who?" Renee asked, coming out of the door with a plate of homemade cinnamon rolls.

"A very attractive retiree who lives down the road from here in Vineyard Haven."

Bitty had been invited to play in a ladies' putters league, which she did twice a week and loved it. She also met quite a few single men who enjoyed taking her out to lunch.

"Renee, you need to cool it on the pastries," Evelyn said.

"I'm sorry, but G is really into buttery, flaky, sugary stuff."

Evelyn sighed, grabbed the warm glazed delicacy and took a bite. She'd never lose those last ten pounds.

"Look!" Renee grabbed the binoculars that sat outside. "There's a whale! Look!"

Sure enough, there along the water's horizon, a whale breached the surface, spraying water out of its blowhole. Tears sprang to her eyes, and a laugh escaped her.

"Are you crying?" Renee asked, rubbing her protruding belly. She could no longer hide the pregnancy.

"I'm happy," she said.

She looked out at Wanda and Bitty, who smiled back at her in a silent acknowledgment of sisterhood. They had each other. She would never have guessed when she got stuck next to Wanda on the ferry or when she first spotted Bitty that their friendship would change her life. If she hadn't stayed, if she hadn't seen that darn seagull, she might be in Minnesota, alone, wishing time away.

"Yes, it's a good day!" Bitty exclaimed.

Wanda rubbed Renee's back. She'd almost taken on an aunt role for her daughter. Wanda had changed the most since they met each other. She had grown quiet over the last month, more introspective and reflective. At first, this sudden change had worried Evelyn, but she realized some of that energy she had first seen had been Wanda's worry and anxiety. Wanda no longer filled the space with words but took in the space with thought. Cancer had strangely given Wanda an inner peace, a strength she hadn't used or known she had before.

Renee passed the binoculars to Wanda and took a sip of tea she had probably made from some organic spice that was said to be good for the baby. Renee no longer did anything unless it was good for the baby.

"You know, I'm pretty happy too," Renee said, blowing on the top of her tea. "I'd be happier if I could get a whole night's sleep, but G thinks he should kick all night instead."

"That never ends, even when your baby's a parent," Bitty said.

Evelyn could see the transformation in Renee as well. When she arrived at the island, she was scared and confused and hurt. Now, as she prepared for motherhood, Evelyn saw her confidence grow. Her happiness with herself increased.

She still worried about Renee. It wasn't going to be easy to be a single parent, and she wasn't going to be around forever, but she had no worries about Renee being a mother. She was going to be a wonderful mother.

She heard trucks pull into the driveway and doors slamming shut. "Mateo and his brothers are here."

"I can't wait for the new stove." Renee clapped.

It was delivery day for some of the new appliances that would be installed in the kitchen. Renee had strongly encouraged Evelyn to go "all in" with the appliances. A beautiful Wolf gas stove with a double oven. A farmer's sink deep enough she could practically take a bath in it. A glass refrigerator she promised to keep spotless, and a deep freezer big enough to store a dead body. "You're not even going to hear the dishwasher."

Evelyn wanted to ask about Chicago, her marriage to Harry, and why Renee left the restaurant, but things had been going so well, and Renee was so happy, that Evelyn didn't want to push it, and worrying about something wasn't going to change a thing. She had a lovely day ahead of her, and she wasn't going to let anything ruin it.

Mateo came around back, and Renee offered him cinnamon rolls.

"We're going to be removing the wall in the kitchen today," he explained one more time. Basically, the ladies had to get out of the way. "And then we will need to shut off the power."

"We're all set for the day." Evelyn didn't know what she was doing, but she knew she wasn't staying at the beach house.

Just as Mateo left, Stan came trotting along the walkway, with Charlie following behind. The dog skipped right up to the deck and into Evelyn's arms.

"Stan!" She kissed the top of his head and pulled out a home-made treat from Renee. "Give me a paw."

Stan sat and put his big paw into her hand and licked her face.

"Good boy!" She laughed as she put the treat into his mouth.

She rose as Charlie approached, and he placed his hand on the back of her waist, drawing her closer to him, and kissed her.

"Good morning," he said, separating slowly from her.

"Good morning," she said back to him, wishing they didn't have an audience.

He pulled a wrapped box from behind his back.

"You brought me a gift?" she asked, jittery with excitement.

He smiled. "Yes, but this isn't for you." He handed it over to Renee.

"For me?" Renee smiled, pulling off the paper. Inside the box was a handmade recipe book. The leather had the title *Renee's Recipes* engraved on the cover.

"This is beautiful." Renee's eyes glistened. "Thank you."

Renee hugged Charlie, and Evelyn's heart stretched with full-ness. She never imagined her heart to be so full after losing so much, but there she was amongst the most important people in her life, and her heart continued to swell in happiness.

As Mateo shooed them out of the house, she took his hand into hers, holding it with both of hers. "You ready?"

She loved her daughter and friends, but she couldn't wait to see what Charlie had in store for them for the next few days. She wondered what kind of gift was coming for her.

"Absolutely," he said, kissing her again.

"They came!" a voice called out from the front of the house. "They came!"

"Is someone here?" Wanda asked.

"They came!" the voice came closer.

Evelyn looked at the house, and from around the corner, Harper came running toward them.

"They came!" Harper held up her phone. "My book edits! They're here!"

She placed the phone in front of Evelyn, a document full of editor's marks on the screen.

"You did it." Evelyn rubbed Harper's back. Harper had been working hard with Evelyn and the editor the publishing house had picked for her. They seemed to be getting along great, and within a few weeks, Harper's book seemed to be almost finished.

"Check it out," Harper said, scrolling after the title page to its dedication.

To Evelyn,

For making dreams come true.

Evelyn immediately covered her mouth as she teared up. "Thank you, Harper." She hugged the new author. "That's so nice."

"I couldn't have done this without you," she said.

"You would've been just fine." Evelyn was sure of it. Harper had a bright future of storytelling before her.

Evelyn looked down at the screen again. Like a balloon inflating, her heart swelled with happiness. Even with all the awards, accolades, and praise on her craft, she never had a book dedicated to her. Nothing felt better than helping another writer fulfill their dreams.

"I'm so proud of you." She hugged the young woman, squeezing her tiny body and swinging her back and forth.

"That's amazing," Renee said, looking over Evelyn's shoulder at the book. "I can't believe you're going to be published at twenty-eight years old."

"I know!" Harper squealed.

Charlie beamed at his daughter, and Evelyn loved seeing that look on Charlie's face—one of pride and love and devotion. Charlie Moran was a good man, a good father, and a good friend, but he was so much more than that.

When he found out Renee was pregnant, he took up a fatherly role with Renee and the baby. He gave her a bassinet he'd made for Harper and helped them put together all the baby's things from three-sixty swings to diaper genies. He ordered books, lots and lots of books, that Renee had asked for so she could read about pregnancy, birth, parenting, prenatal yoga, and anything else to do with the miracle of birth.

"I had hoped to get it before the next writer's group." Harper couldn't contain her excitement. "To share it with the writers' group, but Sue sent it today."

"That's wonderful." Bitty patted Harper on the back. "You should be proud."

Wanda took a picture of Harper and Evelyn, saying how lovely they both looked. The women became noisy, and that's when Charlie tugged at her hand and whispered, "Are you ready for our adventure?"

Evelyn looked out at the crowd of old and young, at her new home, and then back to Charlie. She didn't know what the future might bring, but as she looked into Charlie's eyes, she realized she would be okay not knowing what came next.

"I can't wait."

I hope you enjoyed *Beach Home Beginnings*! In the next book, *Sea View Cottage*, Evelyn's daughter Renee comes to Cliffside Point in need of some motherly love and a fresh start. Click HERE to read *Sea View Cottage* now!

If you'd like to receive a FREE standalone novella from my Camden Cove series, please click HERE or visit my website at ellenjoyauthor.com.

ALSO BY ELLEN JOY

Click HERE for more information about other books by Ellen Joy.

ACKNOWLEDGMENTS

Thank you to my editor Amanda Cuff. Your professionalism, your advice, and the dedication you gave to my story is remarkable. Thank you for your effort on this work. I truly appreciate it!

Thank you to Teresa Malouf for proofreading my story. I cannot thank you enough for what you do for me and my writing career.

Thank you to Tina Durham-Bar. I love that you took a chance on me. You advice, you help, and your friendship has been very cool. Thank you.

Thank you to my first reader, my mom, Kathryn Tomaszek. This book had everything Kathryn, Golden Girls, vacations, bathroom breaks, and everything that reminded me of the Favorite women, hobbies, womanhood, and family. I love being your daughter. I am proud to have you as my mom.

Thank you to my husband, Jay. I love our life. Thank you for everything.

Thank you to my little men. Man am I proud of you two. I love being your mom.

Thank you to my readers. I absolutely love hearing from all of you. If you ever want to write, please do! I love hearing what you think.

ABOUT THE AUTHOR

Ellen lives in a small town in New England, between the Atlantic Ocean and the White Mountains. She lives with her husband, two sons, and one very spoiled puppy princess.

Ellen writes in the early morning hours before her family wakes up. When she's not writing, you can find her spending time with her family, gardening, or headed to the beach. She loves summer and flip-flops, running on a dirt country road, and a sweet love song.

All of her stories are clean romances where families are close, neighbors are nosy, and the couples are destined for each other.

[f]

Made in the USA
Columbia, SC
12 October 2024

44236519R00138